together
apart

together apart

NATALIE K MARTIN

LAKE UNION
PUBLISHING

Published by Lake Union Publishing, Seattle

www.apub.com

Amazon, the Amazon logo, and Lake Union Publishing are trademarks of Amazon.com, Inc., or its affiliates.

ISBN-13: 9781503944114
ISBN-10: 1503944115

Cover design by Najla Qamber

Printed in the United States of America

He who loves you, loves you with all your dirt.
—Ugandan proverb

1.

'arry me, Sarah.' Adam blinked. Had he really just proposed? He had. He'd proposed. Marriage. He'd proposed
marriage?

Sarah's eyebrows shot up. 'What?'

Maybe it was the alcohol. Yeah. That's probably what it was.
The booze must have mixed with the romance in the air and turned
him soft. But then, if that's all it was, why did his stomach sink
to the floor at her reaction? Did he really want to marry her? He
looked across the table at her. Yes. Yes, he did.

'Seriously. Let's get married.'

As he said the words, the idea cemented itself into his
consciousness like an affirmation taking hold. He bounced his leg
under the table. How had this happened exactly? He drained the
last of his beer. The last thing he'd expected was to get sucked in
by the charms of Santorini, with its reputation for sunset weddings
and proposals. He looked at the sky behind Sarah. It was a kaleido-
scope of colours, and after watching the sun dip below the horizon
against a purple and orange backdrop earlier, he had to admit it was
awe-inspiring. The air was still warm out on the terrace of the restaurant, and the view around them was picture perfect, right down
to the cruise ship cutting through the sea in the distance. The place
lent itself to romantic gestures, and now that he thought about it,

proposing seemed like the natural thing to do, even if he hadn't exactly planned on doing it.

'I know I don't have a ring, but we can get one this weekend and make it official.'

It was probably for the best that way. Sarah wore quirky jewellery, like the tiger's eye pendant hanging from her silver chain. He couldn't imagine her opting for a diamond. He moved his chair to sit next to her, held her head in his hands and planted a kiss on her lips. Every nerve ending in his body buzzed with adrenalin, just as they had years ago when he'd done a bungee jump in Thailand. He'd stood on the edge of a water tower, looking down into the blue-green waters of a lagoon, with his heart in his throat and his stomach bouncing with nerves. But as scary as it was, it had nothing on this.

'I love you. I want you to be Mrs Sarah Thompson.'

He told her that he loved her all the time – daily, actually. It had never sounded so important until now, but a look of hesitation quickly passed across her face.

'I don't really know what to say,' she replied.

He smiled. 'Well, it's the first time I've ever done this, so I'm no expert, but I think yes is the universally accepted answer.'

She put her hands on his and took them away from her face, looking around at the other diners in the restaurant. 'I need some air. Can we go?'

His insides nearly fell to the floor as the words left her mouth, but when her cheeks started to blaze red, he let out a sigh of relief. He understood. Of course she wanted to run away from the restaurant. She was embarrassed. There was no way anyone around them could have heard their conversation, but it was obvious. He sometimes forgot how shy she could be. A busy restaurant was the worst place he could have proposed. Thank God he hadn't got down on one knee. She probably would have fainted with embarrassment. He signalled

2

the waiter for the bill as Sarah rummaged around in her handbag. It might not have been the Hollywood-style response he'd expected, but at least she hadn't said no. He put his hand on the small of her back as they left the restaurant and joined the steady stream of tourists.

'Better?'

She nodded. 'Sorry, I just had to get out of there.'

He shrugged, trying to disguise his unease, but nonchalance was the last thing he felt. He'd done this all wrong, launching a proposal at her out of nowhere, especially since she'd told him before that she hated surprises. He had to play it cool. He would wait until they were back in the privacy of their apartment. She liked to be in control of things, and a proposal was a huge step. He understood that she'd need time to process it.

They wove their way through the labyrinth of marbled streets, past the shops selling paintings, sculptures and leather bags, back to their apartment. He took a deep breath and held it in his lungs. He was in the heat of a foreign country, and the salty tang of the sea filled the air around him. The stress of work had been forgotten, and he was relaxed and happy with Sarah by his side. He might have shoved his foot in his mouth and botched dinner with his bumbling proposal, but he still had a smile on his face because at that moment he wouldn't want to be anywhere else.

As soon as he opened the door, the stifling air inside their studio apartment hit him, and he headed straight for the fridge. He took a long swig of water as Sarah went onto the terrace and leaned against the railing. He threw the empty bottle into the sink and went out to join her. She didn't turn around as he stepped out, but enticed by the familiar, fruity scent of her shampoo, he put his arms around her waist and looked up at the sky. Two nights ago, they'd sat on the beach after dinner, and a shooting star had soared above their heads. Sarah had smiled, saying it was romantic. The proposal might not have gone smoothly, but he reckoned it topped the romance scales over a shooting star, and it was a perfect way to end their first holiday together.

He kissed the top of her head. How should he propose for the second time? He could get down on one knee and come out with a heartfelt speech, but that wasn't his style.

'So . . . second time lucky?' He leaned down to kiss her neck.

Sarah turned and put her hand flat on his chest. Why wasn't she looking at him?

'I can't.'

He frowned, trying to ignore the uneasy way his stomach was turning. 'What?'

'I can't marry you.'

Adam took a step away from her as his heart missed a beat before stuttering back to life and hammering against his chest. 'Is this some kind of joke? Because if it is, it's really not funny.'

She shook her head and finally looked him in the eye. 'I'm sorry.'

His breath caught in his throat, and everything around them fell silent, until all he could hear was the pounding in his chest as his heart cracked with every beat it made. A cold sweat broke out on his skin, and the turning of his stomach gave way to a dull, heavy lurch as her words reverberated around in his head.

She'd said no.

2.

dam's stomach churned. The plane lurched, but it wasn't the turbulence making him feel sick. He couldn't stop thinking about the look in Sarah's eyes when she'd turned him down. Everything in him wanted to ask why, but he'd lost his voice, and she'd practically hung off the far side of the bed with her back to him all night, with a seemingly impenetrable wall around herself. It was probably for the best anyway. So far, not speaking to her was working just fine because if he did say anything, he would explode. Or implode, which was much worse. At least with an explosion, the effect of her rejection would be immediate – he would simply burst in a ball of shattered pride. But if he imploded, he would be in one piece, having to feel the confusing, painful and, frankly, embarrassing aftermath of rejection collapsing around him. He shook his head and looked out of the window.

All he wanted to do was get home and put Santorini firmly in the past. He wanted the familiarity of his flat. *Their* flat – the place they'd been turning into their home as they started building a life together. Being back there would put his proposal in context and make things right. It had to. Sarah sighed in the seat next to him and played with the ends of her hair. It reminded him of the first time he'd seen her, the previous autumn.

࿐

After squeezing himself through the closing doors of an Underground train, he'd sat down and leaned over to pick up a newspaper on the opposite seat. When he looked up, he saw her sitting a couple of seats away, dressed in a grey trouser-suit and flat ballet-style shoes. She wasn't his usual type. He normally preferred the typical high-street honey with glossy hair, perfectly applied makeup and a sharp attitude.

For starters, she wasn't wearing a scratch of makeup. Her fingernails were bitten down and unpolished, and her chocolate-brown hair fell in waves around her shoulders. She was toying with the ends of her hair, and when he'd caught her eye, she'd looked surprised, and her eyes had darted around the carriage as if she were checking that he wasn't looking at someone else. It was cute. He couldn't help looking at her over the top of his paper, and the more he looked, the more he liked what he saw. She had something about her that the girls he was used to didn't, and it was that something that had made him stand up as they pulled into Warren Street Station and follow her up the escalator. It wasn't even his stop. He needed to go up to Euston, but he couldn't just let her leave.

He'd followed her through the ticket barrier and croaked at her before they left the station.

'Excuse me. You don't know how I can get to Dover Road, do you?'

There was no way she could. He'd had to think of something to start a conversation with, so he'd made the street name up on the spot. She turned around to face him, and up close he saw the freckles sprinkled across her nose and cheeks against her mocha-brown skin, the bright amber of her eyes and the small, faded scar above her left eyebrow.

She shook her head. 'Sorry, I don't.'

One of her front teeth was ever so slightly crooked, and it only made her more gorgeous. For some reason, still unknown to him, he didn't reply, and he lost the opportunity to carry on the conversation. He must have freaked her out by staring, because she gave him a wary smile, shrugged her shoulders and left him standing there as if she couldn't get away fast enough. He'd been on his way back to the office and decided to walk the rest of the way after grabbing a drink from the café across the road. Sitting by the window, he'd laughed at himself.

After splitting up with his ex, he'd fully embraced single life. Every weekend, he'd go out with his best mate, Carl, get drunk and pull girls. The last thing he wanted was commitment; instead, he concentrated on enjoying himself without the burden of having to answer to anyone else. So why was this girl different? Why had he got so nervous when he spoke to her? He must've looked like a complete moron. Maybe it was because he pictured them laughing over dinner and going for walks in the park. What was that about? It wasn't that he was emotionally devoid; he wanted the same things everyone else did eventually, but settling down wasn't on his to-do list for a few more years.

He'd shaken his head and gulped down the last of his coffee. So she'd made his stomach somersault – big deal. He couldn't sit there all day fantasising about a woman who'd probably already forgotten he even existed. He had a meeting to get to, and the last thing he needed was to be late. As he left the café, he almost stopped walking mid-stride. There she was, heading back to the Tube station. It had to be more than coincidence that he was seeing her again after stopping for coffee at a random café.

As she got closer, he'd taken a breath and stopped her in the street. She might have thought he was a crazy stalker, but who cared? That swirly feeling in his stomach was back. There was no way in hell he was going to let her go a second time.

Sarah sighed next to him as the light behind the seatbelt signs above their heads switched off. This wasn't who they were. This wasn't what they were like. They were the couple everyone loved to be around – his friends had said it enough times. They could spend hours talking about anything. Despite her shyness, she had opinions about everything. Her smile was wide and warm, and her laugh was so infectious, it was difficult not to join in. She could distract his thoughts when he was stressed or annoyed, without him even realising what she was doing. So how the hell were they sitting only inches apart and acting like strangers?

'Do you want anything from the trolley?' Adam asked, breaking the silence as he saw the flight attendant making her way up the aisle.

'Um, just a Coke, please.' She tucked a strand of hair behind her ear.

Her hand was shaking, probably because of the turbulence. He still wanted to comfort her – put an arm around her and kiss her, like he would if things were normal between them – but the wall she'd put up around herself since last night was still there. How was he supposed to talk to her, let alone comfort her, if she wouldn't let him in? She'd turned down his proposal, but it wasn't like they were splitting up. Marriage was a big commitment, and he wasn't going to leave just because she wasn't ready for that step. He could wait. They just had to talk, but she was giving no clues as to when the wall she'd built would start to come down.

She leaned her head back against the chair and breathed out through her mouth.

He sighed. 'Are you okay?'

She nodded and shifted in her seat to face him, leaning on the armrest. 'Adam, listen, about last night . . .'

The woman sitting next to them lowered her magazine, and Adam saw her looking at them out of the corner of her eye. Couldn't Sarah have said something earlier? Like when they were waiting in the airport bar for their long delayed flight to arrive, instead of now, sitting in an aeroplane with minimal privacy and a woman who was clearly eager to eavesdrop sitting right beside them?

'I don't really want to talk about it right now.'

'Oh. Okay.' Sarah nodded and looked away.

Adam looked down at his watch. There were still three hours to go before they were due to land. He closed his eyes and pretended to sleep.

୧∾੭

His head thumped as they exited Gatwick Airport, and the cool air around them as they walked through to the car park did nothing to help. Sarah was silent as she sat in the passenger seat of the car beside him, and he thought about the prospect of the long drive home in silence.

'I can't wait to get home,' he said, putting the key in the ignition. It was a flippant comment, but it was obvious she'd taken what he'd said on the plane the wrong way, and he was beginning to feel irritated with the tension between them.

'Do you want to change the radio station?' he asked as they left the car park.

No reply.

'We should've flown from Luton, really. It'll be ages before we get back.'

No reply.

'Typical to come back to rain, isn't it?' He cringed. Had he really resorted to making small talk about the weather?

Still no reply.

He gripped the steering wheel. She was sulking, but if anyone had that right, surely it should be him.

'Look, Sarah, I didn't mean I didn't want to talk at all. It just wasn't the right time or place,' he said, struggling to keep his tone light. She had always been more guarded than he was, but she'd never withdrawn from him like this before, and he felt like he was trying to coax a cat from a tree.

Still, she gave no reply.

'Sarah? For God's sake, will you talk to me?'

He looked at her as she stared straight ahead. It was like she was on a different planet altogether. She sniffed and leaned her head against the window. Great. She was going to start crying. He tightened his grip on the steering wheel and kept his eyes firmly on the road ahead as they sped home in stony silence.

As soon as they got home, Sarah went straight to bed without even uttering a word in his direction. He sat on the sofa with his mind replaying every detail of the last twenty-four hours. He must have missed something, because it just didn't make any sense. He rubbed his hands over his face and sighed. She'd tried to talk on the plane. Surely, that had to be a good sign? He lay down on the sofa, pulling the blanket across his body. They'd talk tomorrow. Everything always looked better in the morning.

❧

7 September, 5.50 a.m.

I haven't slept at all. The bed feels so big without Adam in it, and I spent all night with my face buried in the pillow because I didn't want him to hear me crying. I've got no right to. After all, this whole situation is my own doing. I'm officially a fuck-up. I'm a horrible, horrible person. The look on his face when I said no – I can't get it out of my head. It was like, in that instant, something in him shifted. I've broken his heart, and, worst of all, I can't bring myself to tell him why.

I wonder if he's awake. The TV in the living room has been on all night. Maybe I could go and sit with him. We could talk and try to salvage something, and I could cuddle up to him, breathing in his smell and twirling his dark hair around my fingers like I always do. I could say it was just a shock, and I wasn't thinking straight.

If only I could. I love him. God, I love him – the very bones of him. But I can't do it. I can't marry him. I had to say no and I know, deep down, that it was the right thing to do, even though it's killing me inside. He'll eventually realise I'm not the kind of person he wants to marry. It'll be better for him in the long run, even if he doesn't know it yet.

I really don't want to get out of bed because when I do, I'm going to have to break his heart all over again. I just wish things could be different.

❧

Adam switched off the alarm on his phone as it started vibrating next to his head. He heard the shower running in the bathroom and slowly sat up, rubbing his neck. He'd spent the night lying on the lumpy sofa, drifting in and out of a twenty-four-hour news channel before finally falling asleep to the latest bulletin about a political uprising somewhere in the Middle East. He should have booked today off. Going back to the office the day after a holiday was always bad enough, but after the botched proposal and a crap night's sleep, work was the last thing he was in the mood for. It wasn't like it was a matter of life and death anyway – not like Sarah's job. Being a social worker was important. People relied on her every day, and she had the power to change a person's life with a single report. Meanwhile, he spent his days managing luxury properties and pandering to people who had more money than sense. Actually, he loved his job, but it didn't suit his mood to admit it.

He yawned as he made his way to the kitchen and flicked on the kettle. When Sarah walked in with her dressing gown wrapped tightly around herself and a towel, turban-like, on her head, he handed her a cup.

'I made you some coffee.'

'Thanks.'

She slowly took a sip and leaned against the cooker. He watched as she ran her finger around the rim of the cup and bit down on her lip, a telltale sign she was thinking about something. He needed to say something to end the silence that was getting heavier by the second.

'So, I think we need to talk.'

She nodded. 'I know. I've been thinking. Your proposal . . . It made me realise that I can't do this anymore.'

Adam drew his eyebrows together. 'Do what?'

'This. Us.'

His heart almost leapt right out of his throat, and his cheek twitched as he willed himself not to show the alarm welling inside him. He had to stay in control.

'Are you serious? Forgive me for being a bit dense here, but things were fine before. Are you seriously telling me you want to split up because I proposed? We don't have to get married; I never intended to put pressure on you. There's no reason we can't still be together.'

'It's not just the proposal.' Her voice trembled as she shook her head, looking down into her cup. 'I just can't be with you anymore. It's not fair to either of us.'

Her words hit him as hard as a punch to the gut, and when she looked up at him, her eyes were filmed with tears. There was no way this could really be what she wanted. She might have said the words, but the trembling in her voice betrayed her. This was Sarah. She wasn't a callous person. There was no way she'd throw away their relationship like it meant nothing, whether it was fair or not.

'I'm going to be late. I need to go.' Her voice hitched, and she put her cup on the side.

'You can't just say that and leave. We have to talk.'

'I can't. Not right now. Maybe later.' She shook her head. 'I'm sorry, but I really have to go.'

She left the kitchen, and he watched her go. What the hell was that? He wanted to hear her reasons. An explanation. Anything. Not to be dumped as if the last year hadn't even happened. So he'd proposed – so what? Wasn't that what you were meant to do when you loved someone? Him proposing made more sense than her saying she wanted out of their relationship straight away without any explanation.

He slammed his mug on the side and headed to the bathroom for a shower. The room was dense with steam, and traces of the scent of Sarah's citrus shower gel lingered in the air. It made no sense. Things had been good between them – really good, in fact. At least, they were for him.

Had she met someone else?

He shook his head. He had no reason to suspect she'd cheated, but it had to be something. Maybe she'd never really loved him at all. Why else would a marriage proposal lead to a break-up? He shook his head again. No. There was no way he'd imagined the way they were together. She loved him; he was certain of it. And besides, it sounded like she was hiding something from him. She could be a bit cagey about things sometimes, but he'd never pushed her to talk about anything she hadn't wanted to.

He swiped his palm across the condensed mirror and looked at his blurred reflection. Whatever she was using as a reason not to be with him couldn't be that bad. He loved her, and he knew she loved him back. As far as he was concerned, that had to be worth fighting for.

3.

Adam opened the door to the penthouse flat and stepped back to let the prospective tenant in. What was his name, again? Something Russian, he was sure. As whatever-his-name-was poked his head around the door to the master bedroom, Adam tried to inject himself with enthusiasm. The penthouse was the star apartment and at sixteen hundred pounds a week, it couldn't be left to sit empty.

'What are the other tenants like?'

'Quiet,' Adam replied. 'Professionals, mostly.'

'Any students?'

Adam was about to reply when his prospective tenant's phone rang. Thankfully, he answered using his full name: Nicholas Aleyev. Adam jotted it down on his notepad. He'd known it was something Russian, and at least he'd be spared any embarrassment about forgetting his name. He looked at Nicholas's loafers, so polished he probably checked his reflection in them every morning. He'd fit right into this place. The apartments started at five hundred pounds a week, and for most of the tenants, it was pocket change. They were the powerhouse of the economy – bankers, lawyers and media types. Some were arrogant tossers who looked down at him like he was something on the soles of their shoes, but the majority were actually quite sound. It was obvious Nicholas would fall into the *arrogant tosser* camp. Adam could tell by the way he turned the corners of his mouth down when he looked in the cupboard at the folded linen. Egyptian cotton clearly wasn't good enough for him. He probably wanted sheets of hand-extracted silk, woven by flaxen-haired virgins in the Himalayas who were raised on a diet of honey and yak's milk. Were there yaks in the Himalayas? He was sure he'd seen a documentary about them once.

'So, students?' Nicholas put his phone back in his jacket pocket and looked at Adam.

The student tenants were mostly from Russia and the Middle and Far East, tenants whose parents paid for their rent annually, and he'd never received any complaints about them. Telling Nicholas that would probably be reassuring enough, but then if he let the apartment today, he'd have to do all the paperwork to go with it.

'On second thought, it doesn't matter. I want to be closer to the West End.'

Adam nodded, although, seeing as they were on Great Portland Street, it wasn't possible to get much closer to the West End. Clearly, his hesitation had put Nicholas off. He shook his hand before leading him out of the block. He'd had the opportunity to get the penthouse let, but he'd allowed it to slip through his fingers, and what was worse was that he didn't care. For the first time in his career, he had no drive. He seemed incapable of doing anything other than asking questions about why Sarah wanted to end their relationship, and they were questions he didn't have answers to. It was a miracle he'd even managed to get this far into the working day at all.

As he sat back at his desk, he clicked through to his calendar and scowled. He'd arranged another viewing for that afternoon, but it was the last thing he wanted to do. He would cancel and rearrange it for next week, when, hopefully, he'd have more enthusiasm. It was better than conducting a half-arsed viewing. The last thing he needed was to get sacked.

༄

7 September, 7.45 p.m.

Why do I do this job? Sometimes it just seems like it's all for nothing. Today, I went to visit Becky, and after weeks of parenting classes and counselling, she's started seeing her ex again. Apparently, things have changed. He's like a different man, and they're trying to make things work – she didn't need my help. I can't even count the number of times I've heard those words before. I saw how she winced when she sat down, and even though I could see the fear in her eyes, I knew she wouldn't admit the truth because she knows full well what would happen if she did. I looked at Kyle as he played with his toy car in the corner of the room, and my heart just sank. I can't see this heading anywhere other than a public law case. Kyle will be just another child in the system, and in a few years, a file with his name on it will probably land on my desk, just like the ones that did this morning. Abuse, drug use, neglect. It's always the same – a never-ending trail of shattered hopes and dreams.

At least it's not just me who feels like this. I had lunch with Ruth today, and she's not doing any better with her cases either. Out of everyone here, she's the only one I'd call a friend. It's nice to have someone to talk to without worrying about coming across as too soft to do my bloody job properly. Of course, she asked how Santorini was, and of course I didn't tell her the truth because if I did, I would have had to explain why I said no to Adam. It would all get too messy.

I suppose work has taken my mind off things, though. I'm just wondering how long I can avoid going home. I finished writing up my reports an hour ago – all I'm doing now is killing time. I even called Claire, like an idiot. Even as I left her a voicemail, I asked myself why I was doing it. It's not like she can do anything to help, and even if she could, it wouldn't be fair to dump my problems on her. I promised myself I wouldn't do that again. Anyway, she's probably living it up in Hong Kong or Dubai, or somewhere equally glamorous.

I can't stop thinking *what if?* What if I'd said yes? What if I'd opened up to him? What if he'd understood and still wanted me anyway? What if he'd never proposed at all? I don't even know why I'm thinking like this; it's irrelevant and I can't let Adam see my doubts. I need him to think I'm just being heartless; otherwise, it'll just make things so much harder. It's better that way, for both of us.

If I'm feeling lost and confused, then God only knows how Adam is feeling.

෮

'So, how are we going to do this?'

Adam flinched at the hard edge to Sarah's voice. When she'd left for work that morning, he'd been convinced that she didn't really want to break up. He'd seen something in her eyes that made him think she was unsure or even bluffing. But now? He looked at her as she stood by the living room door, looking like she'd stepped right out of a boardroom in her smart trouser-suit.

'Do what?' he asked, wishing he could stop the conversation right now. When she'd said they'd talk later, he'd hoped it meant they'd actually *talk*, that she'd explain why his proposal had made her want to split up, but he could tell by the way she was keeping her distance that he was in for major disappointment.

'We're tied into the lease until the six-month break clause, right?'

'You want to move out?' Adam frowned and Sarah shrugged back.
'Well, we have to do something.'

'We could try talking instead of fast-forwarding to this.'

Sarah sighed and dropped her arms to her sides. 'I'm not sure what more there is to say. It's over.'

'Because I proposed.'

'I told you, it's not just because of that,' she replied. 'Things have changed.'

'What things? You don't love me anymore? You don't want a relationship?' He looked at her and raised his eyebrows, hoping to prompt her for an answer. 'What?'

'The second, I guess.' Her voice was quieter, but it didn't falter the way it had that morning.

'Wow.' Adam nodded to himself in disbelief.

How could she have suddenly decided that she didn't want to be in a relationship? She hadn't acted in a way that even so much as hinted at it beforehand. He looked at her again, trying to see how she could have fooled him enough to make him think she was in this for the long haul. Humiliation welled inside him as he remembered the happiness he'd felt walking back to the apartment, despite the botched proposal. He'd fooled himself into thinking she was just shy, that he'd simply unnerved her, but she'd fooled him. And now she was doing it all over again.

He clenched his jaw, fighting to keep his face as neutral as possible. 'If that's the way you want to play it.'

Was he being unreasonable? He'd never seen her act like this before, like it was an effort simply to be in the same room with him. He shrugged and looked away from her. If he didn't, he'd say something he'd regret.

'I'm not *playing* anything,' she replied with her eyebrows scrunched together. 'I'm just trying to be civil. We have to work out what to do next.'

'You can do what you want. Stay, leave, whatever.' He set his face as firmly as he could. Of course he didn't want her to leave, but he didn't want to speak to her if she was intent on acting like this. Besides, he knew for a fact she couldn't afford to leave.

'You know I can't leave. Not right now anyway. I'll start looking into whether anyone at work has a cheap spare room to rent or something. Do you think the landlord will let us break the lease early?'

Adam shrugged. 'Maybe, but we'd forfeit the deposit.'

'Okay.' Sarah nodded back. 'So we'll see what he says, and then I guess we have to wait it out.'

'Wait it out.' Adam echoed her words. 'Anyone would think you're being kept hostage.'

'You know I didn't mean it like that.'

Did he? Since he'd proposed, he wasn't sure what he knew anymore, and his brain couldn't take much more trying to figure it out. He'd loved how uncomplicated things were with Sarah, but now he felt like he'd been sucked back into his previous relationships when drama and stress started to creep in. He peeled himself from the wall he was leaning against.

'What do we do about the bedrooms?' she asked. 'I can take the spare room if you want.'

'Honestly?' Adam raised his eyebrows. 'I couldn't care less.'

He picked up his keys from the coffee table, and Sarah looked at him with uncertainty in her eyes.

'Where are you going?'

'Out.'

'But what about all our stuff?'

He looked around the living room. Pictures sat in their frames, propped up against the wall, waiting to be hung, and the bookshelf they'd bought just before going on holiday still needed to be put together. The flat was still in the process of becoming their home.

When they'd viewed it and signed the lease, all Sarah could talk about was how they'd decorate it and make it theirs. Now she was intent on talking about how to break it all apart.

Adam simply shrugged. Right now, all he wanted was to be alone and to empty his head for a couple of hours. He could imagine that after the conversation they'd had that morning, she'd expected him to press for answers, and he knew his feigned nonchalance must have thrown her, but in a few days, she'd see how unreasonable she was being and she'd change her mind. Time was on his side.

༄

Time might have been on his side, but it was moving slowly. Two days later, nothing had changed, and Adam had taken to stopping in at The Grantley Arms after work – anything to avoid going home to the flat. Since Sarah had started coming home from work late too, he guessed she was doing the same.

'Same again, please, Mel,' he said, putting the empty tumbler back on the bar.

'I'm thinking maybe you've had enough,' Melissa replied, raising her eyebrow. Adam smirked, slid the glass towards her and watched as she filled it with more whisky.

She handed it back to him, and he tilted it towards her. 'Cheers.'

He knocked it back in one go and gritted his teeth as it cascaded down his throat and burned in his chest.

Melissa looked at him with her eyes full of concern. 'How are you doing?'

He hadn't intended on telling her about what had happened. The first time he went in, he'd had a quiet pint, just as he'd wanted, but with each visit, the alcohol loosened his tongue; one word followed another. They'd always had an easy tone to their conversations, and her soothing Australian accent was nice. All he'd said was that he and Sarah had split up, and he didn't really know why. He didn't tell her about the proposal, though. He didn't want the whole world to know how he'd been rejected.

'It's weird. I thought we were solid, but it's all just evaporated.' His words slurred together as he frowned, looking into the bottom of his glass.

'Everything happens for a reason – "Plenty of fish in the sea" and all that.'

Adam grimaced. 'I hate clichés.'

If everything happened for a reason, then what was the reason for their break-up? Simply not wanting a relationship after being in one for almost a year, one that was serious enough to warrant taking the next step and living together, wasn't a valid reason – not to his mind. He'd given Sarah everything, and she'd thrown it back in his face. He'd never mistreated her or given her any reason not to trust him. He'd opened himself up to her, and she'd humiliated him in return.

'I agree they're totally cringeworthy, but they help.'

'Nah. I can be realistic without getting all sappy about it. She clearly wasn't happy being with me for whatever reason. End of.' If only saying the words made it true.

'You don't give yourself enough credit. You might act like a dick-swinging Jack the Lad sometimes, but you're one of life's good guys.'

'Yeah well, you know more about me than you do about her. You're biased.'

Melissa laughed. 'Course I am.'

Adam looked to his right to see one of the rugby regulars approaching the bar. They were friendly enough and always lifted the atmosphere, but tonight their roars of overly enthusiastic laughter were irritating. The rugby player slammed his big, calloused hands down on the bar and grunted a greeting at him. Adam nodded back, hoping he wouldn't try to engage him in sport-related chitchat. He wasn't in the mood.

'What's a guy got to do to get a drink around here?' the rugby player asked with a deep, heavy voice.

Melissa flicked her eyes towards the ceiling and grinned at Adam. 'Guess I'd better go shower someone else with my attention.'

As Melissa swapped banter with the big-handed rugby player, high-pitched female laughter rippled from a corner of the pub, and Adam turned his head towards a group of women huddled around a high-standing table. One of them looked directly at him and smiled. She was cute. If he were single, he'd have offered to buy her a drink without a second thought.

If he were single? He half-laughed at himself. Technically, he was free to do what he wanted. Once upon a time, that would have been enough, but he'd changed since he'd met Sarah, in many ways for the better. Now, the thought of being with anyone else but her simply didn't compute. He wondered if it ever would.

He tasted whisky at the back of his throat, and his stomach turned. It was time to go. He needed to stop drinking, and the only thing he'd eaten was a rubbery cheese sandwich he'd forced down for lunch. He waved goodbye to Melissa and stepped out into the cold air. A scowl set onto his face as he zipped up his jacket and set off towards the chip shop, feeling his mood darken with every step.

For the last two weeks, he'd been sleeping on the sofa since he'd never got round to building the wooden bed they'd bought for the spare room, but his back couldn't take much more. He'd sort it out tonight. To think he'd actually contemplated moving his things into the spare room as some kind of gesture of goodwill. Sod that. *She* could stay in the spare room. She was the one who'd ended it and thrown it all away. She was the one who had turned her back on him, and he was damned if he was going to be walked over any longer.

∽

An hour and a half later, he sat on the sofa eating his chips. Reheating them in the microwave made them taste like cardboard, but he'd been so preoccupied that the plan to soak up the alcohol with food had taken second place. As he squirted more ketchup onto the side of his plate, the front door slammed. He popped a chip into his mouth, put his plate on the coffee table and turned down the volume of the television to concentrate on the sound of Sarah's footsteps. She went from the main bedroom to the spare room and back again, before returning to the spare room. After a few seconds of silence, he shrugged and turned the volume back up.

Sarah eventually came into the living room, and he looked up at her. She still had her coat on, and her hair was wet from the rain outside.

'What's going on?'

'With what?' he said and turned back to face the television.

'Why is my stuff in the spare room?'

'Oh, yeah. I put the bed up, and you were late back, so I moved your things for you.'

'Adam, you've literally thrown my stuff all over the floor.'

He shrugged.

'My clothes, my shoes, my paperwork – everything.'

He looked at her standing in the doorway with her arms crossed. 'Don't be so dramatic. You always rearrange things after I clean up anyway, so what difference does it make? Someone had to sort things out, and it obviously wasn't going to be you. Performing some kind of maid service wasn't a top priority.'

'It's not about maid service. It's just—'

'It's just what? What the fuck else was I supposed to do? Move my stuff just to make you feel better? When you dumped me without even so much as explaining why, you clearly didn't give a damn about my feelings, so I'm done giving a shit about yours.'

She stared back at him and blinked. He'd never sworn at her before. He could usually keep a hold on his emotions, but her coldness was ridiculous. How could she be more concerned about her clothes being on the floor than the end of their relationship? He'd known that moving her belongings like that would provoke a reaction; he just hadn't expected it to be like this. He'd hoped that she'd come home, see the switch around and finally be jolted out of her Ice Queen stance, but she was still as cold as she had been ever since he'd proposed.

'Fine, whatever. But you should know you're acting like a total arsehole.'

'And you're acting like a heartless bitch, so I guess we're even.'

Sarah left the living room, and Adam turned his attention back to the television. He winced as she slammed the door to her new bedroom shut. Maybe that was a bit harsh. He shouldn't have sworn at her like that, but his self-protection barriers were coming up one by one. And yeah, maybe he should have taken more care with her things instead of throwing everything in a heap on the floor, but there was no denying it had felt good. Damn good.

4.

'dam, you have got to snap out of this.' Jenny scowled.
Adam could see her lips moving, but the words sounded far away, as if he were underwater. Friday night poker was well underway, and he was on course to getting steaming drunk. Sitting at the large rectangular dining table, he looked around the room. There was no denying that Carl's bachelor pad was better suited than his place. There was more room, for a start. Bottles of Jack Daniel's and Grey Goose vodka sat at the far end of the table, and cigarette packets were thrown into a loose pile along with a multicoloured array of crisp packets and empty pizza boxes. Carl was notoriously anal about tidiness, but he'd opened the door to his apartment in Crouch End and allowed the poker-related carnage to take place with nothing less than a smile on his face.

The fact that there was a noticeable air of tension in Adam's flat provided the definitive reason as to why their poker night had moved to this desirable corner of North London, but it should be his table littered with booze, fags and junk food. It should be him waving his tipsy mates home in the small hours of the morning before falling into bed beside his girlfriend with a stupidly satisfied smile on his face. How times had changed.

'I still don't get how you've managed to get no answers from her at all,' Jenny said.

'It's not as if I haven't tried.' Adam threw his cards on the table. At this rate, he'd be going home with considerably less money in his wallet than he came with.

'You should tell her to move out.'

'Jen has a point,' Carl said, keeping his eyes firmly on his hand. 'It's not good, you two still living together.'

'I'm not about to use my savings to pay her share of rent on a flat I can be out of in a couple of months. What else am I supposed to do? Throw her out and live like a pauper until the lease is up? Neither of us can afford to stay there alone.'

'It's a tricky one,' Matt said. 'What's your landlord saying?'

'Exactly what I knew he would. We can leave, but the deposit won't be returned unless we stay until the end of the minimum term. Neither of us can afford to lose that amount of money, so we're basically stuck. You'd think I'd have thought to negotiate the break-clause down. I deal with this crap every day of the week.'

'Well, it's not like you planned to split up, is it? As far as I can see, you've done nothing wrong. I could wring her bloody neck,' Jenny said.

'Bit much, no?' Matt replied.

Jenny shrugged and stubbed out her cigarette in the glass ashtray on the table. 'I just can't believe you're being so nice to her after what she's done to you, that's all.'

'Yeah well, I think Mr Nice Guy exited the building the other night. I moved her stuff into the spare room a few days ago, and it did not go down well.'

Jenny smirked and raised her eyebrow. 'It's about time too. Don't let her think she can walk all over you, the silly cow.'

'I feel for you, mate. The sooner you get out of there, the better,' Carl said.

Adam nodded, but when he'd woken up the next morning, he'd felt awful for swearing at her like he did. He couldn't throw her out. Her name was on the lease too, and even if it wasn't, it wouldn't make any difference. He wasn't a total arsehole, despite what Sarah thought. Of course his mates had offered their spare rooms and sofas, but if he still had to pay rent on his flat, then what was the point?

'Maybe it's for the best anyway. When I think about it, I don't really know that much about her.'

'Like what?' Matt asked.

'Just stuff. Like, why she never speaks about her family. I don't think I've ever heard her speak to her mum or any other family members for that matter. And she's not been up to Sheffield since we've been together.'

'So she's not tight with her family; it's not that strange,' Matt said.

'I guess not. But you know what is? I don't even know if she *has* brothers or sisters.'

'Are you serious?' Carl asked, and Adam nodded. 'You've been together for this long, and you don't know if she has brothers or sisters?'

'I know, but whenever I asked her about it, she just said she's not in touch with them, and that's as far as she'd go. I never realised before now how weird that is.'

How the hell had he managed to fall in love with someone he knew next to nothing about? She'd morphed into someone he barely even recognised, and he was starting to think he'd fabricated her character, seeing things as he wanted to see them instead of seeing them as they really were.

'Sounds shady to me,' Jenny said. 'If she couldn't even tell you the simplest of things, you'd never have lasted anyway. I don't know what kind of world she's living in, but she can't just go around behaving the way she has.'

'We all know what you think, Jen.' Adam stood up and went into the kitchen.

He rinsed his glass, filled it with water and took a large gulp. He'd had enough of talking about it. It was bad enough that he'd taken to listening to Adele on repeat like a sad case. Even admitting that to himself made him cringe. He heard footsteps behind him and turned to see Jenny.

'I'm going to head off,' he said.

'Why? Things are just about to get going.'

He shrugged. 'I'm not in the mood. I'm playing like shit anyway.'

'Look.' Jenny sighed. 'I'm sorry for going off on one. It just makes me so angry, seeing you like this. I can't believe how she's treated you. It's the last thing I would have expected her to do. I really liked her.'

'I know you did.'

Jenny came across as being tough, but it was all a front. She could have an acid tongue when she put her mind to it, and his past girlfriends had never really taken to her, but it was different with Sarah. They weren't best friends or anything, but they were more than just two people tolerating each other because of their mutual link to him.

'Don't go. I promise not to say another word about it tonight, but we're your best mates, Ad. We just want what's best for you.'

They'd all known each other since they were kids, and had always stuck by each other. When Carl was thrown from his motor-bike, they'd taken turns keeping him company in the hospital. When Matt and his fiancée, Alice, had their baby girl, they'd all been made godparents. They'd all given Jenny a shoulder to cry on when she'd lost her mum to cancer. They were tight.

'I know, but what's best for me right now is to not talk about Sarah. I'm sick to death of it.'

'Fine. Whatever you want.'

'I mean it. Not a word.'

Jenny grinned. 'Cross my heart, hope to die.'

Three hours later, he staggered up his road, focusing on walking straight. Once they'd stopped talking about his problems, he'd loosened up and actually started to enjoy himself. He'd been so distracted with what was happening to him recently that he'd taken little interest in what was going on with his friends. Matt's daughter had just started walking, Carl had finally finished restoring the clapped out Ford Capri he'd bought a year ago, and Jenny was closer to completing on her new flat. Life had gone on while he'd spent every day moping with the question *Why?* stuttering around in his head like a scratched CD.

His road was quiet. At just past 2.00 a.m., most people were probably in bed or getting sweaty in nightclubs. He approached the detached redbrick and looked up at the flat. The living room light was on – Sarah was still up. The walk from the bus stop had sobered him a little, but he still had to concentrate on getting his key in the lock. He hung his jacket on the coat stand and kicked his trainers off. Should he go straight to bed or stick his head around the door and say hello? In the four days since their argument over the spare room, the atmosphere between them had turned decidedly frosty, and it was a constant balancing act between trying to stay civil and keeping his distance.

He slowly opened the living room door, and his shoulders sagged with relief. She was asleep. The television was on, but the volume was so low he could barely hear it. He looked at her sleeping peacefully on the sofa.

His frustration at their situation was compounded by the inescapable fact that he missed her. Even the annoying things she did, like insisting on sleeping with a window open, even if it was freezing outside, or how she'd tidy things up before he'd even finished using them. He'd got used to her little quirks, but now, the same woman he'd excitedly kissed after signing the lease might as well be a stranger. He should never have proposed. If he hadn't, they'd probably still be together, and he'd be able to lie next to her and slip his arm across her waist.

Her chest rose and fell steadily as she slept with an arm covering her eyes, as if she was shielding them from the light. After sleeping on that sofa himself, he knew she would wake up with a sore neck at the very least. If things were normal, he'd wake her up by planting soft kisses across her neck and collarbone, which was, she'd told him once, one of her favourite feelings in the world. Adam swallowed as warmth rushed down his belly to his groin. If only. He sighed, switched off the living room light and went to bed.

He couldn't sleep. The sex drive that had abandoned him since Santorini had returned, and now he was remembering the tickly feeling of her hair against his chest and her small, brown nipples dangling in his face when she'd go on top. He remembered the warmth of her mouth when she'd woken him up with a blow job, and how she'd looked up at him with her big eyes. He moved his hand down to his boxers, wishing it could have been Sarah's instead.

꩜

A few hours later, he propped himself against the boot of his car and strapped on his shin pads.

'You look rough, mate,' Carl said, throwing him a bottle of water. Adam just about managed to catch it.

'I swear hangovers get worse and worse each time.'

Carl grinned. 'Sign of getting old, that. You all right to play?'

'Of course. When have I ever not been okay to play?' He took a gulp of water. It was hardly the Champions League, but everyone still took it seriously, and it was as good a hangover cure as any.

'With the amount you put away last night, I'm surprised your liver didn't try to escape.'

Adam raised his eyebrows. 'Seriously? *You're* lecturing *me* about alcohol?'

'No, I'm impressed,' Carl replied as he pulled his Arsenal shirt over his head. 'You'll be doing it all over again soon. Nick's back from Afghanistan in a couple of weeks, and I was thinking we should go out on a mad one, get all the lads together and make a proper night of it.'

Adam puffed out his cheeks. 'It's been six months already?'

'Yep. So we need to welcome him back in style.'

'Definitely.' Adam nodded. 'It'll be great to have him back.'

'So he can get back to being my annoying brother? Yeah, I suppose.' Carl shrugged, but Adam knew he was grateful for his brother's safe return. 'A night out might do you some good too. It might get you out of this funk about Sarah.'

'How's that, then?'

'Rule number one: The best way to get over a woman is to get inside another one, my friend.'

Adam shook his head but couldn't stop the smile twitching at his lips. 'Crude as always, Carl.'

Carl shrugged as they walked out onto the AstroTurf. 'It might be crude, but it's also very true, and if I know you, you must be in dire need of getting laid by now.'

'Yeah, you're not wrong there.' Adam nodded and winced. The painkillers hadn't kicked in yet.

He'd jerked off, thinking about his ex-girlfriend whom he'd watched sleeping on the sofa in their shared flat. It was a sentence that was wrong on so many levels, but it had made him realise that if he wanted intimacy, it wouldn't be with Sarah. A night out wouldn't fix everything, but it was a good way to start.

5.

I hate this bloody room. It's too small, and with all my stuff in it, it's like an obstacle course. I feel like a prisoner in here, and to make it worse, it's Sunday – officially the worst day of the week. The hours are stretching out in front of me, and all I have to look forward to is flicking through crap TV on my own while other people do annoying, couple-y things like going for walks in the park and driving out for country pub lunches. Smug gits. I wish today could be like how Sundays used to be, when Adam and I would be smug gits too. I used to go to bed on a Sunday night with a huge smile on my face, wishing there could be just one more day of the weekend left. Now, I wish it would just be over and done with already.

I really don't know how much longer I can handle this. Whenever he's in the flat, it feels like every cell in my body is being pulled towards him. I have to retrain myself to understand he's not mine anymore, and right now it feels like a losing battle. He went out last weekend, came back completely wrecked and woke me up with his banging around. He called me a heartless bitch when I went to see if he was okay. I knew it was the drink talking, but I'm not an idiot. There was more than a hint of truth to it. If only I could tell him that I still love him with every ounce of my being, or that most nights I can't sleep because I miss him wrapping himself around me in bed. I want to tell him that I do want to spend the rest of my life with him, even though I said I don't. Of course, I didn't say any of those things. I just kept quiet and helped him into bed.

I knew I should have left him there. I should have walked away, got back into bed and slept. But I didn't. I looked at him passed out on the bed, thinking about how much I used to love breathing in his smell, even if I couldn't remember what he actually smelled like. And how he used to envelop me in a hug, his strong arms holding me close, even if I'd forgotten what it actually felt like. So I did something I knew I absolutely, positively should not have done. I got into the bed and lay next to him with my head on his chest. It was the first time I'd felt calm for weeks. I stayed there for a long time. I would have stayed all night if I could, but I couldn't risk him waking up. If he did, he would have had a go at me for being a complete headcase, or, worse, he might have cuddled me back.

I have to stick with my decision. I have to keep telling him I don't want him, even though it's like depriving myself of oxygen. I have no other choice. Telling him what happened – what I did – is not an option.

৫৯

22 September, 2.05 p.m.

Claire called me back. Actually, she called the day after I'd left her that stupid voicemail, but I kept diverting her calls. I couldn't avoid her any longer. She was in Shanghai (I knew she'd be somewhere glamorous) and wasted no time in telling me how I'd screwed up – how I should have called her straight away and how I should never have moved in with him in the first place if I wasn't prepared to tell him the truth. Tell me something I don't already bloody know. We ended up arguing, like we always do. I already know I've screwed my life up, yet again. I don't need Miss Goody Two-Shoes to tell me as well.

I should never have called her. I miss her and I love her – of course I do. But our relationship only seems to revolve around disasters. The memories, the guilt, the shame – I can't deal with it. I won't call her again.

∾

Adam watched the unnervingly tall redhead looking around the state-of-the-art kitchen and could almost taste the commission. Things were looking up and not a moment too soon. At work, he was the bee's knees, the dog's bollocks. He'd earned a reputation for letting out the apartments quickly and efficiently, so much so that he'd ended up taking over lease negotiations with the big companies who rented the bulk of their apartments from the managing director, but lately he'd brought his personal problems to work with him, and it was starting to show. Everyone knew all about his break-up, including the contract cleaners. It was embarrassing.

'Everything's included in the rent, right? Including use of the gym and spa?' she asked with her American accent, raising a perfectly plucked eyebrow.

'The facilities and maid service are, but bills aren't. Plus, you'll also get a discounted rate at the hair salon and the florist just outside. You work in advertising, right?' If his memory was correct, she was a director at some massive transatlantic outfit.

'Yes. I'm based mostly in New York, but I need somewhere to stay when I'm over here.'

'This is a great location,' he said, leading her onto the decked terrace decorated with tidy potted plants. 'You have great views, easy access to Regent's Park and the Tube, plus the West End is only minutes away for shopping, restaurants and theatres.'

He followed her gaze and looked at the rooftops sitting under a perfectly blue, cloudless sky. The crisp autumn air settled on his skin. He felt invigorated. Finally, something had clicked. It was over. He wasn't going to act like a lovesick fool anymore. He had an ego to salvage, after all. Carl had arranged their night out for the following weekend, and for the first time in what felt like forever, he wanted to go out and pull. It was as much about getting Sarah out of his system as it was about getting laid.

He looked over the railing and pointed down at the street below. 'And since this is the penthouse, you also get designated parking.'

He looked at the redhead and held his breath. This was why he loved his job – the seconds before the deal was closed, when it could swing either way.

'I'll take it.'

He grinned. Job done. It was shaping up to be a cracking week.

⁓

Later that evening, as he flicked through the channels on TV, his mobile phone vibrated. He'd promised a colleague he'd bring in his Goa guidebook. It was a good thing he'd had the sense to put a calendar reminder on his phone; otherwise, he'd have forgotten all about it. He switched off the TV as Sarah came into the living room.

'I was going to get some take-away after Pilates. Do you want anything?'

'No, thanks,' he replied without even looking up at her.

He listened to her leave the flat and scowled. Spare-room-gate was the last time they'd said more than a sentence to each other, and that was two weeks ago. How much longer could he cope with them living together? He sighed and went out into the hallway. They'd only moved in three months ago, but already the storage cupboard was alarmingly full. He started removing boxes and bags and swore. They were going to have to put some time aside to throw out what they didn't need. It would make packing easier, at the very least.

He finally found the guidebook hidden amongst some old novels stuffed into a holdall and flicked through it, remembering his holiday with his ex. He'd had enough of gaudy European resorts full of endless tacky Irish pubs with pissed-up teenagers and thought that Goa, with its chilled and hippy reputation, would be perfect. It turned out to be anything but. It was the first time they'd had to spend twenty-four hours a day together, and a week in, tempers had flared. Maybe he just shouldn't go on holiday with women anymore. He didn't exactly have a great track record with them.

A red and blue shoebox in the corner caught his attention. It wasn't one of his. He'd probably put it in here by mistake when they moved in, but it was strange that Sarah hadn't noticed. She was meticulous with her belongings. He lifted the lid and frowned at the pile of notepads and school exercise books in front of him. Picking up the one at the top, he flicked through the pages, filled with Sarah's neat handwriting. They were diaries. He knew she kept one, but he'd never considered reading it. It would be a major invasion of privacy. What did she write about now? No doubt it was about him and their break-up. Maybe if he read it, he'd be able to find out why things had turned out the way they did.

He flicked through the rest of the diaries. They seemed to stretch back years. It would be wrong to read them, especially as she seemed to go out of her way to keep her past to herself. He should tell her they were in here, really. She was bound to notice they were missing sooner or later. He shrugged and replaced the box. It wasn't his problem anymore. They were over.

❧

26 September

It's been nearly fifteen years. *Fifteen years.* Already. How is that even possible? For the last few days, that familiar feeling of someone lurking in the shadows has come back. This guilt . . . It's like blocks of concrete weighing down on my chest. Sometimes it's too strong to bear, and I wish I could tell someone, but everything would be ruined if I did – my job, my family, everything. I'm not a heartless person. I know I'm not. If I were, I wouldn't feel like this, and I wouldn't think about him every single day.

I hate feeling like this. I feel so anchorless without Adam. He's gradually slipping away from me, and I can't blame him. All he knows is that I'm acting like a stone-cold, heartless cow, especially after how I acted when he switched our rooms over. It wasn't that I was more concerned about my stuff than what's happened between us; it was just that it was so final. It was as if he wanted to send me a message that he's moving on, and if that's really what it was, it came across extra loud and clear. And I know that I've brought this on myself because I wanted him to accept we're over, and I knew it would hurt, but not like this. It's more painful than I could ever have imagined. Since then, we've barely spoken but, as heartbreaking as it is, at least it's giving me some space to at least try to move on. It's not really as if I've got any other choice. I just have to keep focusing on the fact that it's for the best.

It was so stupid of me to think I could have a happy ending. This is my punishment for what happened, and while I might not like it, I can understand it. I just hate the way I've hurt Adam.

Ruth sent round an invite at work for drinks for my birthday next week. I didn't have the heart to tell her I don't celebrate it. I really do hate this time of year. God, I can't deal with all of this right now.

6.

The door to Carl's flat swung open to reveal Nick's wide grin. 'Go on: get that down your neck.' He held out a shot glass, and Adam raised his eyebrows at the green liquid. It wasn't the usual greeting he'd get when he called round at Carl's, but sod it. If he was going to get messy, he might as well do it properly. He took the glass, necked his shot and shuddered.

'Good lad.' Nick laughed before grabbing Adam's hand and pulling him into a man hug, slapping him on the back.

'Good to see you, mate,' Adam said, trying not to gag at the aftertaste of the absinthe. It was a foul drink, but an obvious favourite to get the night started. He'd picked up a bottle of Jägermeister on the way over – they could keep the green fairy for themselves. As Matt and Jenny got the same treatment behind him, he wandered into the kitchen, where Carl was busy cracking open a can of lager. Music pounded from the speakers, filling the air around them with deep, frenetic bass lines.

'Alright, mate,' Carl said, offering Adam a can.

Adam reached for the bottle of Jack Daniel's. 'I'm good, but I'm not on the beer tonight. I'm going to get messy.'

'Did you bring the Jäger?'

'Yep,' Adam replied, putting the bottle down on the side. He nodded towards the group of guys in the living room. 'Who are these lot?'

'Nick's mates. Some army, some not,' Carl replied, looking over Adam's shoulder. 'Wakey, Tubs, Ryan, Jonesy and Dave. I don't know the others – forgot their names. We're just waiting on a couple more, I think.'

'Pour me a JD, Ad,' Jenny said as she joined them with Matt and Nick.

'I thought this was meant to be a boys' night,' Nick said.

Adam nodded. 'It is. Jen's one of the boys – you know that.'

She never missed a night out, and in her loose vest, skin-tight jeans and high heels, she stood out in the testosterone-filled flat like a lighthouse in the dead of night.

Jenny gave a lopsided smile. 'I'm a special case.'

'Never hurts to have some eye candy, I suppose.' Nick grinned.

'Clearly being at war hasn't knocked the chauvinist out of you yet.' She raised an eyebrow. 'You're about as smooth as a badger's arse.'

Nick winked. 'You know you love it.'

'In your dreams, G.I. Joe.' She shook her head, but the grin nearly leapt off her face. Despite the way they bickered, it was no secret to any of them that she'd harboured a crush on Nick since they were teenagers.

Matt handed Nick a can of lager. 'So, how've you been?'

'Not too bad, you know.' Nick shrugged.

When Nick enlisted for service at eighteen, Adam had been filled with intrigue. He didn't know anyone in the army, and having grown up watching films like *Apocalypse Now* and *Full Metal Jacket*, it had sounded adventurous. So much so that he even thought about joining himself, until Nick was sent to Kosovo. Adam had nothing but admiration and respect for Nick, but he quickly realised that he preferred the safety of being a soldier on his Xbox instead of the real thing. Nick had changed, and it seemed to get more and more pronounced every time he came home. Carl and Nick had always looked alike. There were three years between them, but they were roughly the same height, same build and had the same shade of almost black hair. These days, Nick sported a typical military short-back-and-sides haircut, and his arms were covered in tattoos, but it was the air he carried about him that set him apart. Adam didn't like to think about what he must have seen.

'So, what's the plan? Where are we going?' Adam asked, keen to get moving before everyone got too comfortable or drunk to leave.

Nick looked at his watch. 'We were waiting for Iain to get here, but that tosser's always late. We might as well get cracking. Line up some shots, Carl.'

Carl put glasses on the side and poured out shots while Nick gathered his mates in the kitchen. It was bigger than average, but with twelve of them crammed in, it felt decidedly small.

Nick rubbed his hands together. 'Right lads, on me. Take a knee.'

Adam looked at Carl with a frown. 'Take a what?'

'Take a knee. It means gather round. Listen up,' Carl explained and they all took their shots.

'Christ knows where Iain is, so we're going to head off,' Nick said and wiped the back of his mouth with his hand. 'I thought we'd head into Camden first, hit a few bars and see what's going on before going into town.'

Adam shrugged. 'Sounds good to me.'

'Right, lads. Let's finish up these drinks, grab your cock armour and move out,' Nick said before draining his can of lager.

Adam turned to Carl. 'Cock armour? Move out? What's with all the bossiness and military lingo?'

'That's just Nick.' Carl shrugged as they made their way out of the kitchen. 'And he knows Jen loves it. Tosser.'

Adam laughed as they left the flat and set off towards the Tube station. Tonight was going to be a good one.

❧

'This is so going on Facebook.' Jenny showed him the picture of Carl's post-tequila-shot face.

'You're terrible.' Adam laughed and shook his head. Jenny was lethal with a camera.

'Ah, he'll get over it.' She grinned and put her phone away. 'What about her? She's been eyeing you up since we got here.' She pointed to a blonde girl in a booth by the bar.

He glanced over at her before shaking his head. 'Nah, she looks shy.'

He'd had a year of shyness, and it was more than enough. He wasn't used to shy girls, and he wasn't even sure he liked it. He'd tried it with Sarah and mistaken her shyness to mean she was down to earth and straightforward. How wrong had he been? He definitely wasn't about to make that mistake twice. Tonight, he wanted the complete opposite of shy.

'You can't just disregard girls for looking shy. Have you never heard the saying "A quiet lady on the street is a freak in the bedroom"? "Still waters run deep" and all that.'

'You're insane, do you know that?'

'I'm just trying to get you back to the Adam we all know and love, that's all. You've been acting like such a girl lately, with all your moping about, that your dick's probably shrivelled up altogether.'

'I'm sure saying something like that goes against wing-woman code. What about you, anyway? When are we going to lose you to a successful lawyer type? That's what you city girls go for, isn't it?'

There was no denying Jenny was a good catch. She had a great sense of humour, she was gorgeous and she was quickly working her way up the forensic accountancy ladder. He'd fancied her a bit when they'd first met, but she'd never shown anything more than platonic interest in him, which was just as well. Sparing their friendship the complications of having slept together was what made their connection so tight. It was the same with Matt and Carl too. If any of them had slept with Jenny, the dynamic simply wouldn't be the same.

'I'm not a typical city girl; you should know that by now. Besides, smarmy lawyer types aren't my style. You should know that too. You're a crap friend sometimes.'

'Only sometimes?' Adam grinned. 'What's the deal with you and Nick? You've been stuck to each other like glue all night.'

'I dunno.' Jenny shrugged. 'Nothing, I guess. I mean, he's Carl's brother. It's just asking for trouble.'

'Fair enough.' He caught the barman's eye and ordered two more shots of sambuca.

A smile slowly spread across Jenny's face as the DJ mixed in the next song. 'Wow, this song reminds me of—'

'Kavos?' Adam thought back to their first mates-only holiday and grinned. 'I know.'

'God, can you believe that was eleven years ago already?'

He remembered it like it was last week. Well, some of it, anyway. Their flight had landed at two in the morning, and they'd dumped their suitcases in the hotel before heading straight out. The freedom of being eighteen and on holiday without parents for the first time was electric. They'd got completely hammered, and Matt ended up having to carry an obliterated Jenny back to the hotel. It was a crazy start to one of the best weeks of his life.

'Remember the guy who worked in that bar? What was his name again?' He paid for the shots and handed one to Jenny.

Jenny frowned. 'Which guy?'

'You know – the one with the moustache and the gapped teeth.' They downed their shots, and he shook his head, grimacing. Why did he order sambuca? He didn't even like it.

'Ah.' Jenny licked her thumb. 'Christos.'

'That's right, Christos. He was a total legend. Those cocktails . . .' He pictured the blend of eight different spirits that Christos had served them in tall glasses with mini cocktail umbrellas. That was the night Jenny had got sick.

'Yeah.' Jenny pulled a face. '*Those* cocktails. Ugh.'

'I'm surprised you can even remember his name, you were so pissed.'

'How could I ever forget, with that moustache?'

'It was an epic 'tache, though; I'll give him that.' He looked at Jenny smiling at him. 'What?'

She shook her head. 'Nothing. It's just nice to see you smiling again, that's all.'

'Yeah, well. It's been a good night, so far.'

And it had. Now, all he needed to do was pull, and it would be mission complete.

A trail of lilies etched along Tamsin's spine moved as she danced. Adam had approached her at the bar, and compared to the other women in their short dresses and high heels, she'd looked understatedly sexy in a backless top and skinny jeans. Since then, he'd thought of little else than tracing his finger along the lilies curling their way down from the nape of her neck to the waistband of her jeans.

She was a phenomenal dancer. She really seemed to feel the music, moving her body in a way that filled his head with images of what he hoped would be on the cards later. He put his hands on her hips, and she backed into him, reaching her arms over her head to weave her fingers through his hair as the bass reverberated in the humid air around them. With the dance classics the DJ was churning out and the sweaty bodies thrashing on the dance floor, he almost felt like he was back in Ibiza. He'd worked a season there after university and nearly every night was full of debauchery – booze, girls and drugs. It felt like yesterday.

As Tamsin swayed her hips, he kissed the side of her neck, slipped his hands under the soft material of her top and ran his hands up her sides, letting his thumbs brush the sides of her breasts. It was time to go.

He put his lips to her ear. 'Where do you live?'

'Croydon. You?'

'Finchley.'

She turned around, wrapped her arms around his neck and kissed his lips. 'So, let's go back to yours.'

He was about to nod until the image of Sarah popped up in his head. He blinked it away. 'Can't. My sister's staying with me.'

Did he really just refer to Sarah as his sister? Christ, that was a bit low. But then, he didn't really want to say he was living with his ex-girlfriend. Talk about complicated.

'My place it is, then,' Tamsin replied.

❧

5 October, 4.50 a.m.

There's no point pretending to sleep anymore. Adam still hasn't come home. I went into his room after he left. It smelled of his Hugo Boss aftershave, and there were pairs of jeans on the bed. I bet he's wearing his faded Diesels, the ones that hang on him just right. It's obvious he went out to pull, and judging by the fact that he hasn't come home yet, he's clearly been successful.

The thought of him in the arms of someone else makes me feel sick. I don't want some random girl to touch the smattering of freckles across his shoulders or the bit on the back of his neck that makes him shudder with pleasure. I don't want anyone else to kiss the chickenpox scar on his rib like I did. And I know how much of a selfish cow that makes me sound, but it's how I feel. I even thought about texting him. Half because I wanted to check that he was alright, and half because I thought that if he saw a text from me, he'd feel bad about trying to get with someone else. And then I realised I was just being stupid. With the way I've been acting, seeing a text message from me would probably propel him towards someone else quicker than I could blink.

Maybe he's still propping up the bar somewhere. He *might* not have pulled. In fact, I bet he hasn't. I bet he's in a drunken mess somewhere. It wouldn't be the first time he'd have ended up in a state on a night out with his mates, especially with Carl. The idea of him in an awful state isn't a nice one, but it's better than the alternative.

❧

Adam closed the door to the flat behind him and looked in the full-length mirror hanging in the hallway. He looked dishevelled and tired – not unusual after a night out – but he forced himself to look again. He could hear Sarah in the kitchen, stirring a spoon in a cup. Would she be able to tell that he'd slept with someone else? Was he radiating it without even knowing? Why did it even matter? She wasn't his girlfriend anymore; he could do whatever he wanted with whoever he wanted.

'Good night?'

He turned at the sound of her voice to see her standing in the hall, holding a cup in her hand. Something deep inside him stirred as he looked at her in her little pyjama shorts and T-shirt. The stirring was swiftly replaced by a powerful pang of guilt. He'd had fun with Tamsin. It was exactly how he'd hoped it would be, and they'd swapped numbers to keep in touch, but after hearing Sarah's voice and the strain behind her casual tone, he felt like the biggest arsehole in London.

Adam momentarily looked down at his feet and nodded. 'Yeah, it was alright.'

'Cool.' Sarah nodded back, and they stood looking at each other for a few seconds.

It was moments like this that told him she wasn't any happier with their situation than he was. He could feel the jealousy emanating from her, but what could he do? So far, his plan to let time take care of their situation wasn't working, and all he was aware of was the fact that he hadn't showered before leaving Tamsin's flat.

'I'm going back to bed,' Sarah said, and Adam stepped back to let her pass, wishing he smelled fresh instead of hung-over and carrying the scent of another woman.

She walked past him and into her room, and he looked at the back of the door, trying to ignore the way the guilt had hit him when he'd looked at her. He had to keep telling himself that he was single. She was the one who wanted things to be this way, and the quicker he moved on, the better.

7.

I went to the church up the road after work today to light a candle. I stood in front of the other tea lights with their flames flickering in the air, and the tangy, briny, iron-like smell was so real, it nearly overpowered me. It might have been fifteen years since *that day*, but the memories are as raw as ever.

Bad luck, fate, pure chance. I've tried to come up with a reason as to why it happened in the first place for a long time, but I know that there isn't one. I stood in that church, thinking back to my fifteen-year-old self, heartbroken and terrified, crying to the point of sickness, and told myself that there couldn't be a God. He wouldn't have allowed something like that to happen, to shatter the lives of two teenage girls and strip them of their innocence. But the stupid thing is that I still lit that candle, the same way I do every 15th of October, because for some inexplicable reason, stepping inside the church, feeling the cool air inside its stone walls and breathing in the smell of beeswax makes me feel less alone. It makes me think of Mum. She used to take so much comfort in her religion. I wish I had that. I wish I had her here.

I miss her. So, so much. I just want her to put her arms around me and tell me that she loves me. But she wouldn't understand. Nobody would.

∽

Adam did a double-take when his mobile phone rang in the middle of poker night. He'd just sent a particularly filthy message to Tamsin, and if anything, he would have expected to see her name flashing up at him on the screen, not Sarah's. When was the last time she'd called him? He scowled and diverted the call. Less than a minute later, it rang again, and he looked at the smiling picture of her on his screen. What did she want?

He sighed and put the phone to his ear. 'Yes?'

'Hi, Adam? It's Ruth. I work with Sarah.'

'What's happened?' He frowned, shoving manners to one side as a jolt of unease rippled through him. Something was obviously wrong. Why else would her friend be calling him? He left the others at the table and went out into the hallway.

'She's drunk. Like, really drunk. I'm worried about her getting home.'

That couldn't be right. Her workmates must have organised drinks for her birthday, but Sarah never drank enough to get drunk. He'd never even seen her tipsy before.

'Seriously? She doesn't drink much,' he replied.

'Well, she did tonight. I can't let her get on the Tube like this.'

The distorted sound of people shouting and laughing filtered through the phone, and he pictured groups of friends deciding where to go next. Adam swore under his breath. What did she want him to do? He didn't have his car – he'd left it at home since he knew he'd be drinking tonight.

'She's in a really bad way,' Ruth continued.

He pinched the bridge of his nose and squeezed his eyes shut. 'Okay. Put her in a cab, and I'll sort everything out at my end.'

He gave Ruth his address, hung up and frowned, looking at the phone in his hand. Did that conversation really just happen? Sarah – drunk? Even on holiday, she would have one glass of rosé and nothing more. Getting her to drink the complimentary shot of amaretto after dinner was like trying to persuade a vegan to eat a rare steak. He shook his head, went back into the living room and picked his coat up off the sofa.

'I've got to go.'

'Everything okay?' Carl asked.

'Yeah, mate, I just need to go.'

'Do you want a lift?' Matt offered, standing up.

'No, you're all right. You stay and carry on. I'll nip down to the cab office.'

He grabbed a can of Coke from the table and left, jogging to the bottom of Carl's road. He needed to get home before Sarah did, but it was Friday night. He'd be lucky if he didn't have to wait for long. He walked into the tiny cab office with its scuffed magnolia walls and faded threadbare carpet and was relieved when he was ushered straight back out again. Twenty minutes later, having endured the sickly smell of vanilla car freshener and the tinny sound of Magic FM, he paid the driver and stepped out of the car. The whole drive back he'd pictured pulling up outside the flat to find Sarah slumped against the door, but she hadn't arrived yet. She might not have even managed to get a cab at all – they were notoriously antsy about picking up catatonic revellers. He checked his phone for the millionth time. It had been half an hour since Ruth called him. Where was she?

He paced the living room, looking out through the blinds every time the glow of headlights shone through the window. He swore under his breath at the state of her when she finally arrived. She'd been sick all down herself and in the back of the cab. The driver wasted no time in telling Adam he'd have to pay an extra thirty pounds to have the car cleaned. He lifted Sarah from the back-seat of the car and ignored the angry mutterings as the cab driver snatched the notes from Adam's hand before speeding away.

Once inside, he undressed her, leaving her sodden clothes in a heap on the floor, and scowled as he sponged her face and neck with warm water. Her drunkenness was so out of character, even if it was her birthday. It probably hadn't helped that he'd barely managed more than a mumbled, offhand birthday greeting before she'd left for work, but what else was he supposed to do? He was fairly certain there wasn't a line of birthday cards to give to your live-in ex-girlfriend. Living together was getting more awkward every day, and he didn't know how to act. He was constantly swinging between hating her for the way she'd ended things and missing her. He scowled again. What was he even doing here? He should be back at Carl's, bleeding his mates dry over poker. There was no reason for him to be here, doing this. They weren't a couple anymore – Sarah had made that perfectly clear. She wasn't his responsibility, yet here he was, faithful Adam, dependable as ever, sponging her down instead of being with his mates.

Her head lolled from side to side, and the scowl fell from his face. What was so bad that she needed to get herself into this state? He picked her up, took her to the bedroom and laid her down on the bed. She was going to have the hangover from hell in the morning.

She looked at him with glassy eyes. 'I do love you, you know.'

Adam blinked. For a split second, it was like the clouds that had been following him since Santorini had opened up to let the sun on his face. The rush he felt was better than any high any drug had ever given him, but as she rolled over and promptly fell asleep, a frown etched onto his face. She was drunk. His mind adjusted, and his elation gave way as the clouds came back, thick and grey like dirty cotton wool balls. In his experience, the truth was almost always spoken after a few drinks, but if there was one thing the last few weeks had taught him, it was that nothing good ever came from an assumption. He'd assumed that Sarah loved him enough to want to marry him, that she'd say yes without question, and look what had happened.

He shook his head, put the small bedroom bin next to the bed and her handbag on the chair in the corner. A sliver of pink leather peeked out at him. It was her diary. He'd watched her in Santorini, sitting on the terrace in the morning, writing whatever it was she wrote in there, and he'd thought that she looked beyond beautiful in the midst of concentration. Maybe if he read it, he'd find out whether she really did still love him. Then it wouldn't be an assumption; it would be fact.

He glared at the diary. There was no point reading into what she'd said, no matter how good it felt to hear her say those words. He went to turn off the light, but his finger hovered over the switch. The diary was pulling at him like a magnet. He walked over to the bag and looked at it. It looked so placid and harmless, but he continued to glare at it as if it were his fiercest enemy, like they were opponents, ready to step into the ring and fight it out.

How many chances like this would he get?

୧ꙮ

An hour later, he let out a breath he didn't even know he'd been holding. His heart pounded so hard it made him feel sick as he looked down at the words written on the pages of her diary. The pounding intensified, and he hurled it at the wall. He watched it land on the floor with a small thud. His face burned as he got up and poured himself a three-finger measure of whisky. Since they'd split up, he'd felt like his world had collapsed. He'd made a complete arse of himself, moping around and wallowing in self-pity. And for what? She was deliberately hurting him, telling him she didn't want him, when it was written down in black and white that she did.

It had started well enough. He'd been right all along: she did love him. He hadn't imagined it. In the lead-up to Santorini, he was all she wrote about – how excited she was, how loved up she was, how happy she was. And then it had changed, with no warning and still no explanation.

He gulped down the whisky and winced as it burned the back of his throat. Why would she do this? It was obvious something had happened in her past, but even still, she didn't have to end things the way she had.

He never should have read the stupid diary. Knowing she still wanted to be with him just added a whole new dimension to the already tangled mess in his head. If she wanted to be with him, then why did she turn him down? He shook his head, picked up the diary and went into the bedroom.

He looked at Sarah as she slept. *Fucked up* wasn't the term to describe the situation. It was nowhere near accurate enough. He threw the diary back into her bag and went to bed.

8.

A couple of hours later, Adam kicked the door shut, took Tamsin's head in his hands and pushed her up against the wall. He'd lain awake, staring at the ceiling, willing himself to sleep, but Sarah's diary had fired him up too much. He'd reached for his phone, scrolled through his contacts to Tamsin's name and sent her a text. Within an hour, her fingers clutched at his hair, grabbing fistfuls of it as they kissed in the hallway of her flat. She was looking back at him. Why was she doing that? He squeezed his eyes shut and parted her legs with his knee. Open-eyed kissing implied intimacy, and he didn't want that. Not tonight or possibly ever again. Snippets of Sarah's diary popped up in his head, but as he unzipped Tamsin's jeans, he shoved those thoughts away. Fuck her. Fuck Sarah and her fucked-up diaries. Fuck it all.

~

The next morning, Adam opened his eyes and squinted against the bright sunlight flickering through the blinds. His head throbbed as if someone were ramming a sledgehammer into it. This was bad. He hadn't even lifted his head off the pillow yet.

What the hell was that noise? It sounded like an Apache helicopter taking off. He moved his head an inch and saw a cat, lying prone on the floor, purring. It flicked its tail and gave him an uninterested look before stretching back on its hind legs.

Adam trawled his gaze along the floor to the bin and the slither of latex hanging on the side. He sniffed through a blocked nose and twisted his face at the sharp, chemical tang in the back of his throat. What the hell had he been thinking? No wonder he felt like crap. After shagging Tamsin in the hallway, they'd got pissed, and she'd pulled out a wrap of coke. He hadn't even put up a fight. All he'd wanted to do after reading Sarah's diary was get wasted. If the pounding in his head and churning of his stomach were anything to go by, it looked like he'd succeeded.

He looked at the tattoo on Tamsin's back. It had looked like it was alive, rippling across her back as he'd stood behind her while she was on all fours on the bed. He remembered the rush of adrenalin just before he'd slipped inside her. She didn't hold back with what she wanted from him, and the coke only added to the rush. For a fleeting second, he'd felt like his old self, indulging in reckless sex without the complications of emotions.

His skin prickled with heat, and he pulled the duvet back. He'd grown used to sleeping with a window open, and the after-effect of the coke was making him burn up. He got up and dressed as quickly as he could without passing out or waking Tamsin, and slipped out of the bedroom, quietly closing the door behind him.

He made his way down the creaky stairs. She'd sat on one of the steps last night with his head between her legs. She didn't even live alone. Any one of her housemates could have seen them.

He shook his head, went into the kitchen and filled a glass of water. His mouth tasted utterly disgusting. It had been a long time since he'd had a hangover this bad. It had to stop. He knew what this was. It was self-destruct mode.

'Oh God, I feel like crap. Shoot me now.' Tamsin padded into the kitchen and flopped dramatically into one of the chairs around the table. So much for not waking her up.

'Me too.'

'I don't want to make you hurl or anything, but I've got some bacon in the fridge. I could make us a couple of sandwiches, and we could go back to bed? If you don't have anything else to do today, that is.'

Adam took a gulp of water and looked away. Tamsin was a nice girl. He shouldn't have come round last night. He was too angry, too confused, too *everything*. He'd shagged her, but it could have been anyone. She just happened to be there. It was harsh, but it was the truth. What he'd really wanted was to get back at Sarah, but Tamsin was in danger of becoming collateral damage.

'I can't. I've got a lot on today.'

She smiled and shrugged. 'No worries. Maybe next time.'

'Actually, I think it's best if we don't see each other again. I've just had a really bad break-up.'

He frowned as Tamsin started laughing.

'Seriously? I was offering a bacon sarnie, not marriage.'

'No, I know.' Adam shook his head. God, he must have sounded like an arrogant twat. 'But I really have just had a bad break-up, and I don't think that this' – he pointed to himself and then to Tamsin – 'is a good thing.'

'Okay. Like I said, no worries.'

Adam nodded and put his glass in the sink.

'So,' Tamsin said as she stood up, 'I'm going back to bed. I'll see you around.'

She gave him a small smile and left him in the kitchen.

The cool air rushing through the cab window onto Adam's face did nothing to take the sting out of his cheeks. Tamsin had never given him the impression that she wanted anything more than he was willing to give, which was just as well, because giving anything to anyone was the last thing on his mind. They were both adults, and actually it was one of the more amicable partings of ways he'd had, but even still, he felt like a prick.

Carl had said the best way to get over someone was to get inside someone else, but it wasn't true. It was a distraction, that was for sure, but he was nowhere near getting over Sarah, and the sour taste at the back of his throat was down to more than just the coke. After reading her diary and finding out the things he had, he'd called Tamsin because he'd wanted an epiphany: he didn't need Sarah and he didn't want her. He could move on. So why was he feeling the exact opposite?

He sighed and looked out of the window as they sped along the North Circular. London was still asleep, and it seemed like he and the cab driver were the only people left in the city, like the morning after a zombie apocalypse in a film. He'd been so fed up of the melancholic cloud he'd been under since Santorini, and for a while it seemed as though he was starting to feel better, like he was getting over Sarah. But now? Well, now he was back at square one.

As they turned off the North Circular, the familiar streets of North Finchley came into view, and he asked the cab driver to let him out at the bottom of his street. The fresh air and walk might do him some good and drive away the millions of pins digging into his brain.

When he unlocked the front door, he breathed a sigh of relief. He'd made it home without chucking up in the street. He made his way to the kitchen, dropped a vitamin C tablet into a glass of water and listened to it fizz as he walked back to his bedroom. He sat on his bed and looked into the fizzing water.

The anger he'd felt yesterday had been firmly replaced by a heavy weight of sadness. It was all bullshit. Sarah still loved him. She just couldn't be with him. Why? And why, after everything, did he even still care? Why wasn't he able to just forget it all and move on?

He'd known all along that there was more to the story – that was why. He'd known from the minute she'd turned him down that there was something holding her back – something she couldn't, or wouldn't, tell him. What was it? And who was this Claire he'd read about? He'd never heard of her before, but she was clearly someone important.

He could get the box of diaries he'd found in the storage cupboard, read them and get it over and done with. After all, it wasn't like things could get any worse, and his curiosity about the big conspiracy keeping them apart was more intense than ever.

Screw it.

He went to get the box, barely even trying to be quiet in the otherwise silent flat. With the box in his hands, he went back to bed and sifted through the notepads to find the one with the earliest entry.

9.

THE DIARY OF SARAH COLLINS

26 August 1998

Thank God!! After years of sharing a room, I'll finally have some space to myself. I won't have to wake up with some cheesy pop star's eyes staring down at me from the other side of the room. I can finally have the walls painted in the deep purple that I want. When our friends come over, we won't have to run upstairs in a race to be the one to bag the room first. I can have my friends in my beautiful purple room, and Claire can have hers in her disgusting Barbie-like hellhole. We might look the same, but we're totally different. Being a twin isn't anywhere near as great as people think it is.

❧

Adam blinked and reread the last sentence. What the hell? Claire was her twin? How could he have not known she had a sister? And why would she keep it a secret? He'd always assumed she was an only child. She always sounded so envious whenever he spoke about his brothers, but it turned out she had a sister – a *twin* sister – of her own.

He'd only read half a page, and already he was shocked. If this was just the start, then she'd probably end up feeling like a complete stranger to him by the end of it. She'd lied. Maybe not purposefully, but she'd lied by omission. After reading her current diary last night, he didn't think there could be any more that could possibly change his opinion of Sarah, but now he wasn't so sure.

∾

26 August 1998

For a start, she's a total cow. She thinks she's so bloody perfect, and all she does is get on my nerves. All she's interested in is boys, clothes and makeup. You would think being a twin means I should have a best friend and sister all rolled into one. As if. She thinks she's so much better than me, but she's not. She's a freak, and the sooner I get some space to myself, the better.

I am sad to be leaving, though. This is the only place I've ever lived, and every room reminds me of Dad. I still don't know how Mum could want to leave it. It's all Peter's fault. Ever since they got married, he's been banging on about moving out. He hates our estate, so now I'm supposed to be happy that we're moving into a house with a garden. Big deal! I like living here. I don't know who he thinks he is to just come in and start making all these changes. I hate him!

6 September 1998

Today was the first day back at school. Now we're in Year 10, we're in the upper school building with the sixth formers. It's so much cooler than the lower school. There's a common room (not that we're allowed in there), and everyone just seems so different. I saw some of them smoking at the top of the field. One of them even had a mobile phone! So cool. I really want one. In fact, I'm going to ask Mum if she'll get me one for my birthday. That'll show Hannah. She's been such a cow lately. For a best friend, she's not really holding up her end of the deal. All she's interested in these days is Daniel. It's always 'Daniel this and Daniel that.' I suppose he's cool because he can get everyone into Corporation on a Friday night. His brother works on the door, so they never get ID'd, but it's not much use to me when it's next to impossible to get my curfew extended that late. It's just annoying that Hannah's forgotten all about me while she's wrapped up in him.

I'm always the one without a boyfriend in our group, and it gets on my nerves. I'm always the only one who doesn't have someone to drape myself over. Maybe it's because I don't throw myself at boys all the time, but I always thought it was better to be that way. I don't want to have a random boyfriend. I want someone special.

11 September 1998

I miss Dad. Our new house is okay, I suppose, but I can't go into a room and picture Dad in it like I could in our old flat. When I think about all those times I shouted at him, telling him I hated him, because he'd made me angry, I wish I could take it all back. I always thought heart attacks only happened to old people. It's not fair that he died when there are so many old people out there hanging onto life with hardly anything to actually hang on for.

Mum seems to have forgotten he ever even existed. She took down all of his pictures because she said it hurt too much, but now they've been replaced by pictures of her and smarmy Peter. She's even started going to Peter's church. It makes me laugh. She used to say church was only for christenings, weddings and funerals, not somewhere to pass the time on a Sunday morning.

She doesn't do anything fun anymore, and she dresses differently too. She used to wear jeans and high heels, but now all she wears are long skirts and cardigans. I don't know what's happened to her. She's started to drink a lot too. She drinks the wine in the kitchen she supposedly uses for cooking. I don't think Peter's noticed, but why would he? He hardly ever does anything in there. He said men weren't made to be in the kitchen. He's such a chauvinistic pig!

Whatever. I don't really care, as long as he doesn't try to get me involved in his creepy God stuff. He keeps preaching to Claire about all the *wonderful* things God can do. Hopefully, he won't even bother with me. I want him to think I'm beyond even God's help.

3 October 1998

I started my period today. Whoopee-flipping-doo. I have the biggest headache ever, and now I have cramps too. If that's what having my period does to me, I'd rather not have it at all. I feel so bloated. I hope it's not permanent. Apparently, it can make you put loads of weight on. I'm on the verge of being chubby as it is. I don't need any more weight added. Anyway, Mum had *the talk* with me as if I'm some dumb kid who doesn't know all this stuff already. If she's worried about me popping out a baby, then she really shouldn't be. I mean, has she seen the guys around here? No, thanks. I'll probably die a virgin.

On the upside, I'm having my room painted this weekend, and I've already chosen the colour I want. It's called 'Purple Infusion'. I'm going to stop by The Forum this week and pick up some candles and stuff too. Peter's going to paint it. He freaks me out, he's so weird. The thought of him and my mum together makes my skin crawl. It's gross.

9 October 1998

Okay, so I definitely don't believe in God, but I do believe in fate. I met *the* fittest boy ever today. He's friends with some of the other crowd that hang around at City Hall after school, but I've never seen him before, probably because my curfew is so bloody early that I miss all the fun stuff. Anyway, he's gorgeous. He's got these really bright hazel eyes, and I swear, he looks like he should be in a film or a band or something, not dossing around outside Sheffield City Hall. He has this vibe about him, like he has a really tortured soul he's hiding. He just seems so . . . I dunno . . . aloof, I think. I haven't been able to stop thinking about him.

Anyway, everyone's going to Corporation on Friday night, and he's invited us all back to his house afterwards and I *really need* to be there. I don't know how I'm going to do it, but I have to. Maybe Claire will cover for me. She probably won't, just to piss me off, but I've never met anyone I fancied this much before. I know it's stupid. I heard he just split up with Rachel, and she's gorgeous. Next to her, I'm like the Elephant Man, so even though he probably doesn't fancy me at all, I absolutely *have* to be there.

❦

Claire's going to cover for me! All I need to do now is tell Mum I'll be spending the night at Hannah's and hope she buys it.

This is so exciting!

❦

Adam looked again at Sarah's handwriting. He'd always known it to be long and sloping, but her diary was filled with a scrawl that looked like it was trying to leap off the page, just like the tone of her writing. The fourteen-year-old version of her felt like a jack-in-the-box, ready to jump towards him at any given moment. It was different to the always contained Sarah he knew.

A flash of guilt hit him. She'd gone to great lengths to keep her teenage years to herself, yet here he was, getting an almost first-hand glimpse into them. But his Sarah and the Sarah he was reading about were so different from each other that the guilt barely even seemed to matter. He shrugged the feeling away and flicked to the next page.

10.

Claire Collins: Happy belated birthday, Grunge Head! Hope you're okay and not feeling too bad. It's always hard this time of year :-(How's things?
Sent 17/10 09:54 a.m.

Sarah Collins: You know I hate it when you call me that! Thanks. You too. Things are crap. I'm hung-over. Got wasted last night, puked all over. Feel like death.
Sent 17/10 10:01 a.m.

Claire Collins: Hung-over? You're drinking again?? WTF?!
Sent 17/10 10:02 a.m.

Sarah Collins: No, I'm not 'drinking again'. It was a thing for my birthday with work. I didn't even want to go.
Sent 17/10 10:07 a.m.

Claire Collins: You should have just called me. Please don't start all that again.
Sent 17/10 10:08 a.m.

Promise me.
Sent 17/10 10:08 a.m.

???
Sent 17/10 10:20 a.m.

Sarah Collins: I already told you, I'm not starting anything. What would calling you have done anyway???
Sent 17/10 10:23 a.m.

Claire Collins: It would have been better than getting wasted! Are you still up for dinner next week? Spoke to Mum. She misses you. She wants to know when you're gonna go up?
Sent 17/10 10:25 a.m.

Sarah Collins: Yeah, dinner is fine. I dunno when I'll go. Soon, maybe. I'm going back to bed. x
Sent 17/10 10:30 a.m.

Claire Collins: Okies. Hope you feel better. Will call next week with proper plans. Love you. xxx
Sent 17/10 10:33 a.m.

Sarah Collins: Thanks. Sorry for being moody, I just feel like hell. Speak soon xx
Sent 17/10 10:33 a.m.

11.

Adam stepped into the garage, holding two Styrofoam cups in his hand. The smell of motor oil hung heavy in the air. He stifled a yawn. Sarah's diary had made his brain frazzle, and he'd barely slept. Aside from finding out about Claire, which he still couldn't get his head around, he hadn't read anything more than the ramblings of a teenage girl, and he ended up speed-reading the endless pages about how 'cool' and 'gorgeous' this Richard was. The last thing he'd wanted to do was get up early to get his car inspected, but he'd left it to the last minute, and Carl had opened up a spot for him.

'So, what happened the other night?' Carl wiped his hands on a rag, leaving a smear of oil behind, and took one of the cups from Adam.

'Sarah was wasted. It was one of her workmates who called to let me know. She was completely out of it. Threw up in the cab and everything.'

'Nice.'

'I think she was acting out at me a bit.'

Carl pulled a face. 'Why? She's the one who dumped you.'

'I don't know.' Adam shrugged. 'If this had been a week ago, I wouldn't think anything of it.'

'So, add it to the list of things about her that don't make sense, and move on. It's not like it really matters anyway, does it?' Carl handed Adam his car keys and MOT certificate.

'Thanks for this.' Adam shoved them into his back pocket and took a sip of his Americano.

'Standard, mate, don't mention it. So, are you still banging that blonde chick you pulled the other night?' Carl winked.

Adam frowned. There it was. That horrible, guilty feeling he'd carried around since shagging Tamsin to get back at Sarah.

He shrugged. 'Nah.'

'Why not? She was hot, and for a rebound lay you could have done much worse.'

'I dunno. Just wasn't feeling it, I guess.' Adam rubbed his forehead.

Carl put his cup on the roof of the Peugeot 206 in the middle of the garage and walked round to the bonnet. 'Listen. I know you loved Sarah. She was a nice girl, and you seemed like a golden couple, but, mate, it's finished. You can't go around moping all your life.'

'I'm not moping. I've got enough on my plate with work to keep me in the office for hours on end. I haven't got time to mope.'

'Screw work. You're single now. You can't waste your life working and sleeping. You need to get back out there. Shit happens, but when you fall off a horse, you get straight back on again.' He disappeared behind the bonnet. 'Forget Sarah. And I'm being blunt to give you a kick up the arse. If she doesn't want to be with you, then you're just wasting your time.'

'But she does,' Adam muttered into his cup.

'She turned you down and has barely spoken to you since. It doesn't sound like she's falling over herself to be with you.' Carl looked up at Adam and frowned. 'What happened? Don't tell me you shagged her?'

'Of course not. She was paralytic.'

'All you've been saying since you split is that she turned cold on you. Something must have happened for you to think she wants you now.'

Adam scratched his cheek and leaned against the exposed brick wall. It vibrated as a train sped along the tracks above. Tinny music played from the portable radio on the desk cluttered with paperwork. Carl was so tidy at home, but his garage was a mess.

'She told me she loved me.'

'So? She was wasted. It was probably the drink talking.'

Adam sighed. Carl wouldn't judge him for reading her diary, but having to say it out loud made the whole thing sound sleazy.

'I read her diary.'

'Deep. What did it say?'

'In a nutshell?' Adam raised an eyebrow. 'She never wanted to split up, but for some unknown reason, she had no choice.'

Carl straightened up and grimaced. 'That's a bit fucked up.'

'Tell me about it.'

'So, what are you going to do?'

'What *can* I do? I can't tell her I read it. She'd go nuts.'

No way was he going to tell him about Claire. Carl might be his best mate, but he was also brutally honest, and he'd been the first to tell Adam to pull himself together after their break-up. He didn't want his friends to know the extent of her secrecy because he didn't want to hear them telling him to run for the hills. Especially when, if the roles were reversed, it was exactly what he'd advise himself.

What was he going to do when he uncovered her secret, anyway? He couldn't even begin to imagine what it could be, and the only clue from her current diary was that it involved some guy. But that made no sense. She would have been what – fourteen? Fifteen? It was hard to believe she would still be pining over someone all these years later. Although it *would* explain why she'd turned him down – if she was in love with someone else. One thing he'd realised was just how little he really knew about her. What was to say that she'd never really loved him? Adam's stomach turned at the acrid aftertaste of the coffee.

It sounded a lot more dramatic than a case of lost love, anyway. It sounded like someone had died or something. Had she killed someone? It was a ridiculously absurd thought, but it was the only thing he could think of where she would be utterly terrified to tell anyone. And it would have implications for her job and her family, like she'd written.

Was she really capable of killing another human being, even accidentally? The cold air of the garage wound its way into his jacket collar. He didn't know – that was the honest answer. It was completely at odds with her personality. She hardly even raised her voice when she was angry, let alone displayed signs of violence. But then she seemed to be very skilled at keeping secrets and only revealing the parts of herself that she wanted to. The revelation about Claire was a perfect case in point.

Was he really thinking about this? Sarah – a murderer? The awful thing was, it wasn't outside the realms of possibility. She could be a sociopath or a psychopath or whatever it was called.

He shook his head. He had to stop thinking like this. He was tired, and his mind was overreacting. It just wasn't possible for her to have done something that heinous. Of that he was sure.

12.

A couple of hours later, Adam joined the queue in the shop down the road from his street. He was supposed to be visiting his parents for Sunday lunch, but he couldn't face it. He'd told his older brother about the break-up, and within minutes of getting off the phone with him, their mum had called. He usually popped in to see them on a regular basis, but he hadn't been once since he got back from Santorini. There was no doubt they meant well, but he simply couldn't deal with a barrage of questions. Besides, he was shattered after having to get up so early for Carl to MOT his car, and he planned to sink into the sofa with a stash of junk food and a film.

The person in front of him left the shop, and Adam emptied the small basket onto the counter. His dentist would have a heart attack if he saw Adam's load – chocolate bars, toffee popcorn, nachos and dip and a litre bottle of Coke. Adam told himself that the smile on the shopkeeper's face was a friendly one instead of a knowing one, one that said he'd seen countless other guys in the same position – newly single, angry, confused, fed up and tired.

As he opened his wallet, a flash of brown hair in the corner of his vision caught his eye. He handed the ten pound note to the shopkeeper as he looked towards the back of the shop with his heart choking his throat. It was Sarah – he was certain of it. He could recognise her corkscrew curls anywhere. She hadn't seen him, or if she had, she'd chosen to ignore him. A wave of uncertainty hit him. If it were anyone else, he'd go over and say hello, but it wasn't anyone else. She'd holed herself up in her room since coming home drunk, and anyone would think it had never happened: that he hadn't sponged her down in the bathroom, that he hadn't read her diary. That she hadn't said she still loved him. He swallowed and quickly looked back in her direction. She was engrossed in the label on a jar of something. Nobody could read a label for so long. The familiar rush of humiliation hit him as he grabbed the plastic bag from the counter and left the shop.

He swore to himself as he walked away. How many times was he going to feel like this? Why was he the one avoiding her anyway? If anyone should be feeling embarrassed and humiliated, it was Sarah. She'd acted like a total stranger since Santorini and come home steaming drunk. He'd cut his night short to help her out, and she hadn't even acknowledged it. He stopped walking and stood in the middle of the pavement. She'd hidden her twin sister from him, for God's sake. Why the hell was he still being so nice?

Adam looked back towards the shop before leaning against the low wall of someone's front garden. They'd been skirting around each other in what could only be called an attempt at civility to make their messed-up living arrangement bearable and he was tired of it. He was tired of feeling guilty for sleeping with Tamsin, tired of trying to second-guess Sarah, tired of trying to pretend she hadn't hurt him. Maybe it was time she felt some of the awkwardness he was feeling too.

He waited for her, watching a pigeon peck at a half-eaten chocolate bar. The way it pecked away at it was so simple, and he sat engrossed watching it, admiring its determination. If only everything in life were as simple to deal with. The faint bell of the shop door opening and closing made him look up, and he saw Sarah step out. When she saw him, she momentarily hesitated, but it wasn't as if she could turn and walk in the opposite direction. Adam stood as she approached, and he plastered something like a smile onto his face.

'You stocking up too?' he asked, looking at her bag. Through the thin plastic, he could see that she'd gone for a similar selection to his. Of course she had. Pig-out Sundays were something they used to do together all the time.

'Yeah,' she replied, holding it up.

A few seconds passed as they stood on the pavement looking at each other. How could it be so awkward between them when they'd been together for so long? Adam had to remind himself that he didn't really know her, and he was sure her diaries would reveal a whole lot more than a secret twin.

'I saw you inside, so I thought I'd wait.'

Sarah had the good grace to blush, and he knew then that he'd been right. She had seen him, and he took a small bite of satisfaction, knowing that she must have been a little embarrassed about ignoring him.

'Thanks,' she mumbled, and they started walking back to the flat.

The instinct to hold her hand almost took over as they walked side by side. It would have been the natural thing to do, but instead, Adam gripped his bag with one hand and stuffed the other into his pocket.

'So,' he said, 'how are you feeling?'

She looked up at him, momentarily confused before a visible cringe passed across her face. She looked straight ahead and nodded.

'Better. I meant to say thanks. For looking after me.'

'No problem,' Adam replied. At least she'd said thanks. 'That was some state you got yourself into. Was it like a birthday treat?'

'No.' Her voice was sharp, as if he'd said something he shouldn't. 'I don't do birthday treats.'

'It's just as well. Last year you had the flu; this year you got wasted,' Adam said as they approached their building. 'Not having much luck on the birthday front.'

'I don't really celebrate it. I told you that, remember?'

He did remember. Last year, he'd planned to take her to the theatre and a posh dinner, but she'd fallen ill the night before her birthday and cancelled. She wouldn't even let him come over to the flat she was living in at the time, saying she preferred to be alone instead. And there he was, thinking she was uncomplicated. He held in the bitter laugh bubbling in his throat as he unlocked the communal door.

'There's always next year,' he said, following her up the stairs. Based on the last two birthdays she'd had, he dreaded to think what would happen on the next one.

'Yeah. There is.'

He frowned as she unlocked the door to their flat. By the tone of her voice, anyone would think he'd suggested she jump from a plane without a parachute. He'd clearly said something wrong, but before he even had a chance to think about what it might be, she went straight into her room and closed the door.

Adam shrugged his jacket off and shook his head. Getting any information from her was like trying to have a conversation with a lamp post. He went into his room, shut the door behind him and reached for the box of diaries under the bed. They didn't need to talk. He was certain her diaries would tell him everything he needed to know.

13.

Last night was bloody *amazing*!! I wish I could bottle it up and keep it forever.

I spent the pocket money I've been saving and bought a new denim miniskirt and purple tights and teamed them up with my favourite vest top and Converse trainers. Hannah did my makeup for me when I got to her house. She's really good at it, and she plucked my eyebrows too. All I can say is, *Ouch!* But it was totally worth it. I looked at least seventeen, and I felt great.

As soon as we got into Corporation, I felt the adrenalin rush. I was so worried we'd get ID'd, but thanks to Daniel's brother, they just let us straight through. Richard was already there with some of his friends, and when I saw him standing by the cloakroom, I thought I was going to pass out there and then.

In the few seconds I looked at him before being dragged through the club by Hannah, I took in everything – the way his cheeks dimpled when he smiled and how the UV light bounced off his teeth, and how he strummed his fingers against his leg in time to the music as if he were playing a guitar. He was wearing baggy, dark jeans and a brown Airwalk T-shirt, and his hair kept falling into his eyes. I wanted to run my fingers through it. Every single thing about him just screamed sexiness, and my heart thumped in my chest so hard I was sure he'd be able to hear it. Thank God he was talking to someone, or he would have seen me gawping at him like a total lunatic!

After a while, I went to sit in the chill-out room. I was hot and knackered out from jumping around to Greenday and Foo Fighters. The room was dark, with a few sofas dotted around the edge, and I could just about make out a couple fooling around on one of them. All I could think was, *Wow.* Corp was undeniably cool. Everyone wore what they wanted, danced how they wanted and didn't seem to give a toss what anyone else thought. There were Goths and girls dressed like Fifties pin-ups, and there was even a half-pipe where the skaters whizzed up and down. It seemed like the more outrageously dressed you were, the better. My vest and skirt combo felt a bit lame in comparison. It was nice to be surrounded by people who were into the same things I am.

At school, unless I'm with my friends, I always feel self-conscious. I'd shed my pedal pushers and Reeboks in favour of baggy jeans, dog collars and Vans trainers more or less overnight, and it sometimes feels like I'm seen as a bit of a circus freak. I never realised it before but I guess it all started when Dad died and I started listening to his old music tapes and CDs. He was into classic rock, which I found a bit lame, but it made me feel closer to him. I guess it was just a natural progression for me to start listening to the harder stuff. Now I like everything from grunge to metal. I do listen to the chart stuff sometimes. It's hard not to when Claire belts it out from her stereo all the time. After the music, the dress sense followed, and I started hanging out with Hannah and her group of friends. We'd hardly ever even spoken before, apart from in English, where we sit next to each other. I always thought she and her friends were a bit weird, but they're actually the nicest people I know. Not once have I been made to feel like I don't fit in.

So anyway, I was thinking about how lucky I was to have such a great group of friends, when Richard came in. My heart literally skipped a beat, and I prayed that he'd sit down next to me. He did, and when he spoke, I swear, it was like eating a massive bar of chocolate and having my throat stroked with a feather at the same time. I could feel myself tingling all over. We talked about music, films, everything. He's so easy to talk to.

I didn't dance for the rest of the night. I didn't move at all. I was scared that if I did, I'd turn around and he wouldn't be there anymore. I couldn't believe he was giving me the time of day when there were so many pretty girls around. I nearly had to pinch myself to check I wasn't dreaming. I was in Corporation, finally having a night out with my friends, and I was talking to the fittest guy I've ever seen. He's only a year older than I am, but he's so mature, and he was genuinely interested in what I had to say.

I could have sat there talking to him all night, but we had to leave to go back to his house. We ended up walking because we missed the last bus. It must have taken an hour or so to get there, and it was freezing cold. Usually, I'd have bitched and moaned, but I didn't even care. He was walking beside me, talking to me, and then he held my hand! Just like that! Like it was the most natural thing in the world. I can't even begin to describe the feeling when he did but it was *amazing*. His hands were so hot against my cold ones, it felt like they'd burn right through my skin, and he didn't let go the entire way.

His house is huge. It's detached, and his room in the loft is bloody massive. His parents must be really cool to let him have all his friends back to their house. There were about eight of us there, and everyone paired off before passing a couple of spliffs around. I'd never smoked before. I was always too afraid it would make me feel sick, and I didn't want to become some loser stone-head, but I didn't care. It was obviously something Richard did all the time, and I didn't want to look boring. So I took a toke and held the smoke down, trying to make it look like it was something I did all the time and not cough. Of course, I did. I couldn't help it, but instead of laughing at me, he just smiled.

I'll be honest: I didn't really like it. It tasted really gross, and I didn't like the way it made me feel all light-headed, but when he leaned over and kissed me, it didn't matter. I couldn't believe it. It still feels like a dream, thinking about it now. It was perfect. I've kissed a couple of guys before, but they weren't even in the same league. I could taste the weed on his tongue, which wasn't so great I guess, but it didn't matter. *He* was kissing *me*! I felt like I was on top of the world. We kissed all night in between smoking and listening to music.

I've never had such a perfect night, and I doubt I ever will again. My skin is still buzzing. For the last few hours, I've had him kissing me, stroking my arms, my stomach and running his fingers through my hair. It feels like I'm being starved now that I'm home. I need to shower, but I don't want to. I want to savour this feeling before I have to wash it all away. I'm so glad I started this diary. If I wasn't able to read back on it, I'd convince myself I dreamt it all. But I didn't. It really did happen.

I hope he'll be at City Hall tomorrow. I have no idea if this means we're going out or not. I really hope so.

◦◦◦

13 October 1998

Richard was out today. My legs turned to jelly when I walked towards City Hall and saw him sitting on the steps, speaking to Tom. My mind went totally blank. I had no idea what to say to him. I've heard before how everyone pulls each other when they're out, but it doesn't mean they're together. It's just seen as a bit of fun. I'd have died if it had all turned out to be nothing more than a fumble. I sat with Hannah and forced myself not to turn around and look at him. I didn't want to look desperate, just in case. When Daniel turned up, she went off with him (as usual), and within seconds Richard was there, right next to me.

We're together – there was no doubt about that when he kissed me there and then for everyone to see. Hannah can keep Daniel. Richard trumps him in the cool stakes, and he's better-looking too. I can't bloody believe it – Richard Stone is my boyfriend!! I'm so happy! I wonder if it's too soon for it to be love?

14.

Adam closed the gate behind him and made his way through the neat front garden. His parents had lived in this house all his life, and it was comforting to know it was a constancy he could depend on. Once he closed the gate behind him, he would be at the front door within eight paces, and come next summer, the exterior walls would be repainted in the same creamy colour they had always been. The house was repainted every two years, whether it needed to be or not. The three-bedroom semi contained all of his childhood memories, and when he put his key in the door and flicked his wrist with just enough force for it to open, he instantly relaxed.

'Adam?' His mum, Angela, appeared by the kitchen door, holding a roasting tray in her hands. 'I was wondering where you'd got to. Come on – everyone's waiting.'

Rubbing his hands together to thaw out the cold, Adam looked around, and a smile played on his lips. No matter how many times he came through this door or what mood he was in, it always made him feel better. Walking past the stairs and family photos hanging on the wall, he remembered the time when he'd slid down the banister too quickly and fallen, chipping a tooth. Every room in this house had a memory in which he or his brothers, David or Joe, had hurt themselves. They were typical boys growing up, forever scraping knees, bumping heads or splintering themselves on the rough blocks of wood their dad would bring home.

'Here he is.' His dad, John, smiled, lowering the corner of his newspaper. 'So nice of you to join us. We're all starving here, you know.'

'Sorry, Dad.'

Adam kissed his mum on the cheek, and after slapping both of his brothers on the back of the head, slid into the empty chair at the table. His stomach rumbled loudly. Now that he was sat in front of the table piled high with food, he realised just how hungry he was.

'Look at you,' John said, folding his paper in half. 'You're so thin, I could pick you up by those collarbones like a suitcase.'

He looked at his dad's hand. He was sure the tremor hadn't been there before. It seemed like every time he came to see his parents, he noticed something new. More liver spots, more grey hairs. They'd always been fit and active, and they still were, but they moved much more slowly now. The idea of them losing their mobility and getting older . . . He didn't like it.

'Hardly,' Adam replied, reaching into the bowl of roast potatoes and popping one in his mouth.

'Now, Dad, we all know how much care and attention our Ad puts into his physique,' David said, flicking a pea in Adam's direction.

David and Joe were short and stocky like their dad, whereas Adam was tall and lean, taking after their mum. It was a running joke that, next to them, he always looked underfed.

'Leave him alone, John,' Angela said as she placed the gravy boat on the table and sat down. 'He's fine just as he is. Now, let's eat. It's been sitting on the table long enough as it is. You know I like to have Sunday dinner at three o'clock on the dot, Adam.'

Adam, David and Joe mimicked their mum in unison before tucking in and bickering about who had the most food on his plate.

Adam looked at his brothers and smiled. It was nice for them to all be together. Nowadays, they only saw each other for family get-togethers and the odd Sunday dinner, and while they didn't always get on, their family unit was tight. What was Sarah like with Claire nowadays? Since he'd never heard Sarah talking about her, they obviously weren't close. When was the last time Sarah had seen her, or her mum?

'How are Deina and Celina? Still in Rio?' Joe asked, pushing his glasses further up the bridge of his nose. David's wife had gone back to her native Rio for two weeks and taken their daughter with her.

David nodded. 'Fine, considering. They fly back tomorrow.'

Joe shook his head. 'It's awful. The first time Deina goes home in ages, and it's for a funeral.'

'What can you do? People are killed every day in that shit heap.' David shrugged.

'Language, David.' Angela frowned, and he raised a hand apologetically. 'And you should have a little more compassion. I have to say, it looks terribly hard from what I've seen on the telly. All those poor people living in – oh, what were they called again, John?'

'Favelas,' John mumbled.

'Yes, favelas. She's lucky to have escaped that place. Poor girl.' Angela pursed her lips. 'And I'm not happy about little Celina being somewhere so hostile.'

'I have plenty of compassion,' David replied. 'Yeah, they're my in-laws, but it's not like I can do much from over here, is it?'

As the eldest, David had asserted his authority over Adam and Joe when they were younger. It was always a case of what David said went. He could be bossy, selfish and cocky, but he was also funny and loyal, and he stood up for what he believed in. It was to him that Adam and Joe would go for advice growing up, and he was far more approachable than their dad, who preferred knocking things up in the shed to dealing with the raging hormones of teenage boys.

'What about you? Still shackled to your kitchen sink?' Adam asked Joe, swiftly changing the subject. David was always defensive, and Adam could feel his frustration emanating across the table. He had always hated being told what to do.

'Ha, funny,' Joe replied, deadpan.

Joe was the wild one, or at least he used to be. If there was a party going on, he would be there, and if there was some coke or pills doing the rounds, that was even better. Adam would go out with him sometimes and was always amazed at the sheer amount of narcotics Joe could get through. He'd take cocktails of uppers, downers and all-rounders like it was nothing. If their parents ever found out, they'd have matching coronaries. Adam had always been sure Joe would be dead before he reached thirty, convinced he'd be found overdosed in a pool of his own vomit in a crack den somewhere. Until marriage tamed him.

Once again, Adam felt a weight in the pit of his stomach, and it wasn't the food that he'd so hastily eaten. Sarah had slotted in so easily with his family. His dad had liked her in his quiet, reserved way, and his mum had welcomed her with open arms. As the only unmarried son, it was no secret that his parents wanted him to follow in his brothers' footsteps. Then, the Thompson set would be complete – all married off and settled down, leaving his mum and dad to enjoy their retirement without worrying about their wayward bachelor son. They'd probably thought it was a dead cert with Sarah.

He thought about Joe, stuck with a woman who practically held him hostage and demanded all of his attention, all the time, and David, married to a woman so out of his league it was like watching a five-a-side team taking on Manchester United. Sarah had always let him do his own thing, and he'd never felt any pressure to keep her living in a superficial, materialistic bubble.

He hadn't told them that he'd proposed because he couldn't imagine telling them how she'd turned him down. It just wasn't working out, he'd told them. They weren't stupid. He knew they could all see how much he loved Sarah, but he refused to budge, and when they saw that he wouldn't offer up a legitimate reason, they let him be.

Feeling eyes on him, Adam looked to his right. His dad was smiling at him. He wasn't big with words, but he always seemed to know when something was up with one of his boys. The smile was as if to say, 'I know you're not doing so great, but everything will be okay.' His dad had a way of making him feel better without saying anything at all. Adam returned the smile and tuned back into the conversation that was now centred on Mrs Betts, the lady who'd lived next door since the dawn of time and was now moving into a nursing home after having a nasty fall.

'Can you believe it?' Angela asked as she gathered the plates from the table. 'She has two children, both earning disgusting amounts of money in the City, and she has to go and live in a poxy nursing home. I'm telling you right now, I'll never forgive any of you if you do that to me or your father.'

'Mum, she's almost ninety years old,' David said. 'She can barely walk. She can't be rattling around in that house forever.'

'That is not the point, David,' she said, standing by the archway between the kitchen and the dining room. 'Young ones today just don't want the responsibility of looking after their parents. When I get to the stage where I need someone to wipe my bottom for me, I'd rather it be flesh and blood than a faceless, temporary nurse who couldn't give two hoots.'

'Mum! Would you stop it?' Joe said, and Adam laughed at the horror etched into his brother's face.

'Come on now, Ange. We're hardly decrepit, and my bottom is fine, thank you very much.' His dad rose from the table. 'I'm going to the shed.'

David and Joe looked over at Adam and nodded upstairs. Even now, they couldn't resist heading up to David's old bedroom and smoking out of the window. It was stupid. As if his parents didn't know that they smoked. They knew everything. All the times they'd sneaked into the house drunk after a party and thought they'd got away with it, his mum and dad would pull them up on it the following morning, when they were in the grip of cider hangovers. When Adam used to steal a glance at the porn magazines he had stashed in the bottom of his drawer, his mum would come knocking on the door. His parents had a radar for everything that went on under their roof. Adam signalled that he would be up in a minute and picked up the rest of the clutter from the table.

His mum smiled as he put the plates and cutlery on the worktop next to the sink. 'Thanks, love.'

'How's things, Mum?'

'Oh, fine,' she replied, rinsing a plate before putting it in the dishwasher. Adam frowned as she held the small of her back when she straightened up.

'Here, I'll do it.'

'I'm not past it yet, you know.'

'I never said you were.' He held his hands up in mock defence. 'How's Dad?'

His mum wiped her hands dry on a tea towel. 'He's fine. Happy in that shed of his. You don't need to worry about us – we're fine.'

Adam nodded. 'I'm not. It's just . . . well, you know.'

'We're getting old?'

Adam looked at his mum, seeing past the ageing woman she had become to recall the fresh face from his childhood. He shrugged.

'We're only going to get older, God willing.' Angela smiled. 'Go on. Your brothers are waiting for you.'

Adam laughed and kissed her on the cheek. She'd never say it, but he knew he was her favourite. She'd always let him get away with more than David or Joe.

How had Sarah coped being estranged from her family? Sure, his parents nagged and got on his nerves at times, but he knew how lucky he was to have them. It was a shame that Sarah didn't have the same, and he intended to find out why.

15.

'Mr Madsen, I've already called the plumber, and he'll be dropping round today,' Adam said, cradling the phone between his shoulder and ear.

It had been one of those days when everything went belly up. He'd already had to deal with a flooded basement, and between bollocking a cleaner for smashing a bottle of a tenant's perfume and having to deal with the disappearance of the wayward handyman, an angry tenant was another problem he didn't need.

'It's just not good enough.' The voice on the other end of the phone was jarring, making Adam grit his teeth. 'I'm paying nine hundred pounds a week. I shouldn't have to come home to a leaking shower. I don't think you appreciate how difficult it is trying to sleep with a constant dripping noise coming from the next room.'

Adam pressed two fingers against his left temple. 'I will personally see to it that the shower is fixed today, and I'll call you as soon as it's done.'

'I don't know what it is you think I do all day, but I don't have time to sit around and wait for you to call me. I expect it to be done by the time I return this evening, and if it isn't, then I'll be forced to break the lease.'

The phone disconnected, and Adam slammed the handset down, puffing out his cheeks. His shower dripped by itself too sometimes, but he wasn't screaming down the phone at his landlord to fix it. He just ignored it. Which was just as well since his landlord had officially become the most difficult person in London to get hold of.

What was it with these tenants? If turning into a spoiled, over-demanding prick was what came with high-ranking status and having people pander to your every whim, then he'd rather stay where he was. He loved his job – he really did – but on days like this, he wanted to walk out of the office and never come back. With a sigh, he picked up the phone and punched in the handyman's number. All this and it was barely even lunchtime. It was going to be a long day.

◡

25 October

I'm meeting Claire for dinner tomorrow. She's on downtime for ten days, so we'll be able to catch up properly. Nervous isn't the word. It's been ages since I last saw her. I love her to bits – she's my sister. It's just that I always feel so inadequate next to her. She was always so perfect growing up. She was the thinner one, the taller one, the smarter one. Watching her swan around the house made me feel like the ugly duckling – the ugly duckling who messed things up and became the evil twin. But even though I want to hate her sometimes, I can't, because she was there for me. Claire, who could annoy me to the point where I wanted to smash my own head in, was my rock back then. She never judged me, not once. We used to be so close when we were young, and then Dad died, and it all fell apart. But she still supported me when I needed it the most. And now I'm in a mess again, like a moronic idiot who can't learn a single lesson in life.

Argh! I can't be thinking about this right now. The office is starting to fill up, and I've got tons of work to do, which is just as well. At least being busy is saving me from the embarrassment about Friday night. Nobody said anything mean, but somehow I don't think I'll be on the invite list for the next trip to the pub. Oh well.

⚬

Later that evening, after a long, hot shower, Adam flopped onto his bed. It had been a trying day, but everything had been sorted. The leaky shower was fixed, and the elusive handyman had been located. Best of all, the lease on the penthouse had finally been signed, lifting from his shoulders the burden of having their star apartment sitting empty. He was looking forward to the hefty commission coming in his next pay packet.

The sound of the TV echoed from Sarah's bedroom. She must have come home while he was in the shower. For a fleeting second, he wondered if he should go and say hello, but he knew she'd be passive. Sometimes, when they did cross paths in the flat, she had such a pained look on her face that it almost physically hurt him. After the day he'd had, he couldn't deal with feeling dejected too. Instead, he reached under the bed and slid the box of diaries towards him. At first, he'd been paranoid that she had some secret way of arranging them, so she would know if anyone ever read them. He still felt guilty. He was invading her privacy, and she was only a few feet away. Reading them was wrong, plain and simple, and if she ever found out, she would never forgive him, but he just wanted to know what had happened to her.

It had become so much more than uncovering a secret. After the dinner with his family, he'd thought constantly about David and Joe. Their wives were nice enough, but he didn't want to end up like his brothers. Sarah had never made him feel trapped. He was smart enough to recognise a good thing, and despite there being a whole list of things about her that he'd been ignorant about, what they'd had together was good. It was better than good.

❧

19 October 1998

I'm *finally* seeing Richard tonight. He's taking me out for my birthday. I haven't seen him since last week, so we've been mostly speaking on the phone. We're going to watch a film and then go back to his. He's so lucky to have such laid-back parents. There's no way I would ever be able to bring him back here. Peter would go berserk, and I'd never hear the end of it. He goes on at Claire all the time because of the way she dresses and the friends she hangs around with. He keeps saying they're a bad influence, hanging around on the corner of the street even though they don't really do anything other than talk. Mum doesn't say anything. She just lets him preach at us.

I honestly don't know what she sees in him. For a start, he's butt ugly, and all he ever goes on about is Jesus this and Jesus that. He's actually talking about going to Jerusalem next year for a holiday. I mean, *really*?! My friends get to go to Spain and Cyprus for their holidays. I've never been abroad before, and I don't want my first holiday to be some kind of pilgrimage. So not cool!

Anyway, I need to get this maths homework done. I want to be able to totally focus on my first real date with Richard, not worry about bloody Pythagoras theory. I don't see the point in learning this stuff. As if I'm going to need to know about the calculations of a triangle after school! So lame!

20 October 1998

Argh!! Can I not get any bloody privacy in this place? I'm going to go mad, I swear!

Peter read my diary! Of all the lowlife, nosy parker things he could have done. I forgot to hide it before I left yesterday. Who the bloody hell does he think he is? And what was he doing in my bloody room anyway?

I'd had such a great night, and then I came home to see him and Mum sitting at the kitchen table waiting for me. He called me a harlot. Can you believe it? What kind of an insult is that? He's so ancient! He must be from the Dark Ages. Nobody says 'harlot' anymore.

I told him he had no right to go through my things, and he said he could do whatever he wants because this is 'his house'. Apparently, he went into my room to take my clean laundry in and saw my diary on the bed – like that's any excuse. I told him I didn't want him touching my clothes, and he called me ungrateful. And then he grounded me for lying about last Friday and 'taking drugs'. It's not like I've been shooting up heroin – it was only a bloody spliff! God, he makes me so bloody angry! And Mum just sat there, letting him speak to me like that. I don't know what's happened to her. It's like she's become a total sap. She just lets him do what he wants while she gets quietly drunk. Well, he can just do one and fuck right off.

Anyway, back to the important stuff. Last night was brilliant! I met Richard in town, and we went to see a film. I can't remember which one – it was some boring action film – but it doesn't matter. I didn't get to see much of it since we were too busy kissing. I still can't believe I'm going out with him. He's just so gorgeous and so cool, and he has the cutest smile I've ever seen. It's ridiculous. And his hair is so soft, and it flops into his eyes all the time. It makes me breathless just thinking about it.

His parents weren't home when we got back to his. I don't think they're around much from what he told me. Lucky him. Last week, everything happened in a bit of a haze. I was so overwhelmed that he'd even shown an interest in me – not to mention a bit stoned. This time we were completely alone and sober. He has a huge collection of CDs, and he put one on. I don't know who it was, but it was soft and moody and made everything feel so intimate. We spent all afternoon in his bed.

We didn't have sex, obviously. We've only been together for a week. But we fooled around. I thought about tossing him off, but I didn't. I've never done it before, and I didn't want to look like an idiot by getting it wrong, but when I left to come home, I regretted being so chicken. I really, really like him, and I'm certain he likes me just as much. He didn't even try to persuade me to have sex with him. I mean, hello? He's obviously really sensitive and mature because I'd bet money that most boys would have tried their luck with a girl in their bed like that. I know he respects me.

So, massive decision: I'm going to have sex with him. I've decided he's The One. I don't know when, seeing as I'm being held prisoner by that prick Peter, but I am going to do it.

༄

A ball of jealousy tightened in Adam's chest as he looked at the picture of Sarah and, presumably, Richard, wedged into the spine of the diary like a bookmark.

She wasn't at all what he'd imagined her to look like at fourteen. She was chubby, her curly hair was dyed dark red and her piercing amber eyes were rimmed with black eyeliner so thick she might as well have painted her eyes shut. But her smile seemed to leap off the photograph towards him. It was the same smile that he'd fallen in love with.

Richard looked like a Kurt Cobain try-hard, all moody and anguished-looking with scruffy shoulder-length hair. It was obvious from the way Sarah was smiling at him in the picture just how much she adored him. He was her first love. Adam wished it could have been him. She probably wouldn't have looked twice at him back then anyway. As a teenager, he was always the boy the girls liked as a friend but never wanted to get with. He lagged well behind his mates until, apparently overnight, he grew four inches and his skin cleared. Suddenly, he'd had a queue of girls asking him out.

Sarah had been enraged with Peter for reading her diary. There was no doubt he'd be in line for a severe bollocking if she ever found out that he'd done the same, but he was getting closer to finding out the truth. He could feel it.

16.

Adam's eyes flicked from Jenny to Carl and back again. He'd never seen her look so sheepish before.

'Tell me you're joking.' Carl looked at Jenny with his eyebrows pulled tightly together. 'For fuck sake, Jenny.'

Adam glanced sideways at Matt who gave a barely imperceptible shake of his head that said, *Don't get involved.* Adam didn't intend to. He looked down at his cards. Whose hand was it? They were barely an hour into their poker game, but it had stalled.

'I knew you'd react like this.' Jenny leaned back in her chair.

'Well, what else did you expect? He will treat you like shit,' Carl said slowly, like he was talking to a child.

'I'm a big girl. I can deal with it.'

'Right.' Carl chucked his cards on the table. 'And when he screws you over and you get hurt, then what? Because that *is* what will happen. It's what he does.'

Jenny shook her head. 'You don't know that.'

'He's my brother. I know him back to front.' Carl scowled.

Adam could see Carl's dilemma. Jenny was his best friend; Nick was his brother. It put Carl in an awkward position, and even though it had been painstakingly obvious on their night out that something would happen between them, nobody had expected

Jenny to turn up tonight and say that she and Nick were actually seeing each other.

'But you don't know what he's like with me, and he respects that we're best mates. He's not going to jeopardise that.'

Carl gave an exasperated sigh and stood up. 'I don't want to talk about this anymore. Do what you want, but don't come crying to me when he cheats on you, or forgets you even exist.'

Jenny watched Carl storm into the kitchen and groaned with frustration.

Matt whistled. 'You can't blame him, Jen.'

'It's not like I'm doing this on purpose. I don't want to argue with him; he's like a brother to me.'

'Really?' Adam pulled a face. 'Because Nick is Carl's brother. So that would be like incest.'

Jenny rolled her eyes. 'You know what I mean. This isn't some stupid fling.'

'He's just being protective,' Matt said. 'It's understandable. We all know what Nick's like, and even if that weren't the case, he's a soldier. He's hardly ever here. Have you thought about how you'll cope being an army girlfriend?'

'No, because I'm trying not to doom it all before it's even started. Will you talk to Carl?'

'I'm not getting involved,' Matt replied, holding up his hands as he stood up.

Jenny raised an eyebrow. 'Seriously?'

'Yes, seriously. This is family stuff. I'm steering well clear.'

Matt left the two of them at the table, and Adam looked any-where but at Jenny. She was one of his best friends, and he wanted her to be happy, but the last thing he wanted, or needed, was to get involved in a spat between Jenny and Carl. Both were stubborn and both liked to have the final say. Jenny smiled at him.

He shook his head. 'Before you ask, the answer's no.'

'We're meant to be best mates.'

'Don't even try and pull that one. Matt's right, Jen. This is family stuff.'

'Yeah, but you can get through to Carl.'

Adam looked away, shaking his head again. Jenny moved until her face was in front of his.

'Please?' He looked into her eyes and felt his resolve slipping away. '*Please*, Adam. I wouldn't ask if it wasn't important. I really like him.'

How did she do that? She was usually so assertive, borderline aggressive even, but this was in complete contrast to the side she showed to the world. The only other time she'd asked him for help was after her mum died.

'Fine. I'll speak to him.' He sighed as Jenny threw her arms around his neck. 'But I'm not making any promises, and I'm not getting involved any more than that.'

'Thank you.'

He couldn't see her smile, but he heard it. He remembered what she'd said weeks ago. They were best mates, and they always looked out for each other. It was time for him to return the favour.

∽

After Jenny and Carl's argument, poker night was a non-starter, and Adam went straight back home, eager to catch up on the latest instalment of Sarah's teenage rebellion. He looked down at the diary, covered with doodles of hearts and stars, song lyrics and stickers. Sarah was adamant about her relationship with Richard, just the same as Jenny was about hers with Nick. Both had the potential to destabilise relationships around them – Jenny's with Carl and Sarah's with her family. Both of them were headstrong, and maybe that's why Jenny had warmed to Sarah in a way she hadn't with his other exes. Despite their outward differences in terms of personality, they were probably more similar than either of them thought.

∾

3 November 1998

I hate Peter. I absolutely hate him. I've been grounded for two weeks now, and I still have no idea when it will end. I haven't been allowed to go anywhere except school. I haven't even been able to go to City Hall on the way home, so I haven't seen Richard, and to make it even worse, I've been banned from using the phone, so I can't call him. He probably thinks I'm not interested anymore. I asked Hannah to tell him I was grounded, so hopefully he will have got the message, but if he ends up dumping me because of this, it'll be all Peter's fault and I'll never forgive him.

6 November 1998

I *still* don't know when I'll be allowed back out. It's like he's trying to keep me hostage, and I'm so over it. He even times how long it takes for me to get home from school, so I'm expected to be back by 4.30, do my homework and then what? Watch TV? Go to sleep? I'm so bored that I've worked my way through my entire film collection, and I've watched *The Craft* about a billion times already. I've literally never been so bored in my entire life – it's driving me crazy!

25 November 1998

This really is taking the piss now. It's been three weeks. Talk about overreacting! I've decided enough is enough. I used the last bit of my pocket money, which has been stopped while I'm grounded, to call Richard from the payphone. It was so good to hear his voice, but I couldn't speak to him for very long. I only managed to get out of the house in the first place because we needed some milk. I told Richard I wanted to see him. Peter can go to hell. What's the worst he can do anyway? He's not my dad, and he never will be. I don't have to listen to anything he says. I've played by the rules and waited for him to get over himself, but he's taken it way too far. He's going to see I'm not some stupid little girl he can boss around.

26 November 1998, 3.50 p.m.

Claire was less than impressed when I left her in town to come to City Hall after school. She hates Peter too, but she never stands up to him. She just lets him moan at her and never reacts. She says it's better to be that way, and I shouldn't let him see that he's getting to me, but it's easy for her to say. She's not the one who's been grounded for three weeks for no bloody reason. Everyone seems to have forgotten that he was the one in the wrong. He had no right to read my diary. So what if I lied about staying at Hannah's? So what if I went to a club and had a bit of a smoke? It's not like I do it all the time – it was only once! Whatever, I just don't care anymore. Richard means too much for me to lose him.

I know it's crazy because we haven't been together for very long, but I'm convinced he's The One. I'm certain of it. I've always held back when it comes to boys, instead of throwing myself at randoms until now, but I've finally found the one for me. I think about him *all* the time. I even dream about him. All I want is to be with him, and I'm not going to let anyone stop me. Especially not Peter.

I hope Richard gets here soon. Now that it's getting colder, people aren't hanging around for too long, so there's only me, Frank and Rachel here. Out of everyone, they're the only ones I don't really get on with. Rachel hates me because I'm going out with Richard, and he only ever had eyes for her until now, and Frank is like her lapdog, so he stays away from me out of loyalty to her. Still, it's better than sitting alone on these cold, stone steps.

26 November 1998, 8.30 p.m.

Surprise, surprise. I'm grounded again. I'd like to know how that works exactly, since I'm already grounded in the first place. Peter was beyond angry that I'd stayed out after school. He reckons I need to be disciplined. I nearly laughed in his face when he said that. If he even so much as thinks about trying to discipline me, he'll regret it. I got a wicked buzz of satisfaction when I saw the look on his face as I walked in the door. Claire said she covered for me and told him I had drama club after school, which is bloody hilarious, considering that I haven't been in drama club since Year 7. The stack of favours she can call in from me is growing by the day.

After he'd finished bleating on at me, Mum came up to my room and asked why I always had to be so difficult with him. All he wants is for us to be a happy family, apparently. Ugh. I actually had to remind her that I'd never lashed out until he'd read my diary, even though I've never liked him, and he never does anything for us the way that Dad did. She said I needed to give him a chance and how he's really not that bad. She said I was overreacting about the whole thing, but I know full well that if it had happened to her, she'd have gone mental. Just because I'm fourteen doesn't make my feelings or privacy any less important.

I can't even speak to her anymore. We used to be so close until she met Peter. After Dad died, she made an effort to make sure we had time together. Saturday would always be our day, and she would take me and Claire to the cinema, ice skating or shopping. It was fun. But then Peter came along, and she dropped us like hot potatoes.

It's not even like he makes her happy. She seems so miserable all the time, and I'm sure she's becoming an alcoholic or something. She's never totally drunk, but I'm not stupid. She gets all shaky and fidgety and snappy, but as soon as she starts cooking dinner, her mood totally changes. I've noticed that the bottle of red wine in the cupboard has been replaced at least three times in the last few days. Peter never makes out like he knows about it, but it would be hard for him not to have noticed. He's probably making it his mission to 'save' her. She was never like this when Dad was alive.

I miss him so much. Everything was so much better when he was here. Why did he have to go and die? He wouldn't have grounded me for this. I probably wouldn't have even had to lie about going to Corp in the first place. He was so laid-back, I bet he wouldn't be trying to tell me what to do all the time and grounding me just for doing normal teenage stuff. He would have liked Richard – I know he would. And that's why I'm going to do the complete opposite of everything Peter tells me to.

Claire says I'm crazy. She doesn't think any boy is good enough for her to fall out with her family over, but what does she know? She goes chasing after boys, but she never actually does anything with them. That's why, out of all the girls she hangs around with, no one could ever call her a slag. She won't pop her cherry with just anyone, but if she had a boyfriend like Richard and did the things we did last week, she would totally understand. She would get what it's like to have a gaping hole in your heart because you can't be with the one you love.

Yes, that's right. I love him. I'm going to go to his place on Tuesday afternoon. I can't see him this weekend because he's going to visit his grandparents in Cumbria, so Tuesday it is. I've got double maths for my last lesson, but I'm going to skip it, and he said he'll skip his too. His parents will be out, and I'm going to sleep with him. I can't see the point in hanging around. I know he's perfect for me.

1 December 1998

Only one day left! Tomorrow will be my last day as a virgin. I'm so nervous! I wonder what it will feel like. These are the times when I wish I was closer to Claire so I could speak to her about it.

I could always talk to Hannah, I suppose, but we're not as close as we used to be, and so far, she's refused to say if she's slept with Daniel. We're supposed to be best friends, but she's going around acting like she's the only person in the world to ever have a boy-friend. Like it's all so sacred and special that she couldn't possibly share anything with me. So I'll just have to wait until tomorrow and find out for myself.

I'm scared!

17.

26 October

So, I met up with Claire earlier and told her everything – even the thing I've been too scared to write down in case I jinx myself. Experience has taught me there's no point in hiding anything from her. I didn't realise how much I'd missed her, and right now I feel like I can take on anything. It's funny. When I speak to her on the phone, I feel guilty for what I put her through and the memories of that night overpower me. But when I actually see her, it's totally different. As soon as she hugged me, it was like a weight had been lifted.

Of course, she's still the same old Claire – she always thinks she knows best. She still thinks I need to tell Adam everything. She said he deserves to know the truth, and she was majorly pissed off when she realised that he doesn't know anything about her. She just said, 'He doesn't know about me, does he?' It was a rhetorical question. She knew the answer. What could I say to that? I felt awful. How could I tell my twin sister that I've denied her very existence for such a long time? The only consolation was that she knew why I did it. She's the only person who knows what happened. It would have been awkward for the both of us because even though we argue, she'd never betray my trust. She would have protected me, and to do that, she would have had to lie to Adam. He would have been curious about why we hardly see each other. Even her busy flight attendant lifestyle can't explain why we're not as close as twins should be.

She was raging with me. I could see the fire in her eyes, but she didn't flip out. She just pleaded with me to talk to him. I wish to God that I could, and sometimes I do wonder if I've over-dramatised the whole thing. But then as soon as I think that, the guilt comes pouring down. I can't be flippant about it. That would make me a monster, and I really don't want to believe I'm one of those.

It was nice to see her again. Considering she lives in London too, she's hardly ever here. She's always flying off here and there, and when we do meet, I just want to keep her close. I know I let my paranoia take over sometimes. I let myself believe that I'm her dirty little secret, but I know it's not like that. She offered to lend me some money to pay for the rent until the lease is up, so I can move out, and it's tempting, but there's really not much point. We won't be here much longer, and besides, I'm not ready to wrench myself away from Adam just yet. The thought of moving out is like a punch in the gut.

We spoke about other things, of course. Mum's doing fine, still with bloody Peter. I know I'm going to have to haul myself up there soon. It's not fair on Mum to visit so rarely, and I really miss her. And Sheffield. I never thought I'd ever say that.

Heavy rain lashed against the window, waking Adam with a start, and goose bumps spread across his skin. He lifted his head and looked down at himself. He was lying on top of the duvet with only a towel wrapped around his waist and Sarah's diary still in his hand. He yawned and picked up his mobile, squinting at the screen. It was two thirty in the morning, and everything was silent except for what sounded like a fox raiding a bin farther down the road. He got up, pulled on a T-shirt and boxers and headed to the kitchen.

He'd dreamt about Sarah, and as he set about making himself a hot chocolate, a frown spread across his face. All he could see were faint images of her face that slipped out of his reach before he could remember anything else. He rarely remembered his dreams, but he really wanted to remember this one.

He looked down into the cup, took a sip and grimaced. What he'd wanted was sweet, thick hot chocolate, but instead he'd ended up with something that looked like dirty dishwater. When Sarah made it, it would be creamy and frothy, and she'd usually put a couple of marshmallows on top for good measure. He'd forgotten about that.

He made his way back to bed, thinking about the little things she used to do. Sometimes, she would leave little notes tucked into the pocket of his suit jacket. They were never sonnets or profound declarations of undying love, but they were always sweet, often contained a joke and always managed to put a smile on his face, regardless of how badly his day was going.

Did she ever leave random notes for Richard to find? Did she ever make him a mix tape of her favourite songs? She'd chosen him to be the one she gave her virginity to, which was clearly a big deal for her. More than it had been for him. He'd lost his to a girl called Charlotte when he was seventeen. They'd been at a house party and ended up in one of the bedrooms on a bed full of coats. He'd always remember the rhythmic, chafing noise as his leg rubbed against someone's jacket while he was on top of her.

It was selfish and irrational, but he hoped Sarah hadn't made those little gestures of love to Richard. He'd rather think that they were something special and unique – something she'd only done for him.

⁓

2 December 1998, 11.30 a.m.

Today is the day. It's actually happening! Omigod! I am so excited! I hardly even slept last night because I was so nervous, and today is going so slooooooooooow. Physics is beyond boring, but at least I get to write in my diary and daydream about Richard without anyone interrupting me. I just hope no one sees me sneaking off. I haven't told anyone about this, not even Hannah. I want to keep it to myself. This is one of the most important days of my life so far. I just hope it's everything I'm dreaming of.

2 December 1998, 5.30 p.m.

That's it! I'm not a virgin anymore. I did it. I actually did it. It was really nice. Painful, but nice. It felt weird when he met me at the bus stop. We both knew what was going to happen, but we didn't talk about it. It was a bit awkward, and I kept wondering if maybe he'd changed his mind, but when I went into his room, it was obvious he'd prepared. He didn't light any candles or anything lame like that, but his room was super clean, and he'd put new sheets on the bed. He put a CD on, and we sat on the bed for what felt like forever as I waited for him to do something. I was too scared to make the first move.

He was so sweet and took things really slowly. He didn't rush me or make me feel like I was stupid for not knowing what to do. It hurt at first. A lot. In fact, I kind of wanted him to stop as soon as he'd started, but he said it would get better. I mean, it wasn't like it is in films, with both of us being really into it or anything, but he says it'll get better over time. I wanted to ask how he knew that for sure, but I don't want to know how many other girls he's slept with. I'm certain he slept with Rachel, but I don't want to know about anyone else.

Even though it hurt and I didn't know what I was doing, I wouldn't change it. Having his naked body against mine . . . just amazing. And what was great was that I didn't feel insecure about my body, not even once. We cuddled and talked afterwards. I can't even really remember what we spoke about. I was in a bubble of happiness. All I could think was how right it all felt. It was everything I've ever dreamt of, and I know how lucky I am to have lost my virginity to my boyfriend, who I love. I bet not many girls get to say that.

So, I'm really sore now, but I can't stop smiling. I'm like a deranged clown. Even Peter's ranting as I strolled in an hour late didn't bother me. His moaning just bounced off me like an echo.

3 December 1998

I told Claire about yesterday. I hadn't planned to, but it was a secret that felt too big to keep. I mean, hello, it's *huge news*! I had to tell someone, and even though we don't always get on that well, she *is* my twin. She was so shocked, especially because we've only been together a little while. She hasn't done it yet, so she wanted to know everything. I didn't leave anything out, and her eyes got wider and wider with every word I said. They got so big, they almost took over her entire face – they were like saucers!

It was really nice to speak to her like that. We hardly ever talk about anything properly. She's always out with her friends, and I'm always in town with mine. It reminded me of how things used to be, and I think, more than anything, she likes that I'm standing up to Peter. I always thought she just didn't care that he's waded his way into our family and is trying to take over. I told her I was going to do what I wanted from now on, no matter what Peter says, and the look on her face was priceless. I don't think she thought I had it in me.

4 December 1998

I nearly told Richard I love him today! I chickened out, though. I think he feels the same way, but I know I'd just get my words all mixed up and look like an idiot if he didn't say anything back. I'm going to stay over at his house this weekend, and it can't come quick enough!

∾

Adam put the diary down. He'd struggled to read about her first time. It was like he'd crossed a line somehow. It would have been different if she'd told him herself, but this was something she'd written for her eyes only. He felt like a voyeur.

He remembered the anticipation he'd felt the first time he'd slept with Sarah. After a month of dating, he was crazy for her, but what surprised him was that he'd really wanted to take things slowly. No matter what anyone said, sex changed everything, and those first four weeks had been perfect. If things were going to change, he'd wanted them to change for the better. It had finally happened after a night out at a comedy show. The laughter was a definite aphrodisiac. Even now, just thinking about her throaty laugh made his groin stir.

Images of her from that night floated in his mind – stills, frozen in time, like a photograph. Like how her hair tumbled around her shoulders when she'd released it from the ponytail it had been tied up in, and how her skin glistened with sweat, like it was covered with diamonds. He'd licked the soft skin under her breasts and kissed the delicate crease in the crook of her elbow. He'd stroked the silkiness of her inner thighs and traced the line of four tiny magpies tattooed on the side of her hip.

He'd explored every inch of her, and it wasn't just physical. He'd looked into her eyes and seen the very same emotions he was feeling reflected back at him – lust, love and even fear. There was no going back from that moment. That was when he knew he was hooked.

Adam shook his head. The truth was, the idea of proposing to her had been lurking in the depths of his mind for weeks before he'd found the courage in Santorini. If he'd never found the nerve, everything would be how it used to be. He'd be in bed with Sarah, sleeping soundly after having almost-guaranteed Friday night sex, instead of sitting up at nearly three in the morning, reading her diary like a sad loner. But then again, he wouldn't have found out about Claire – or the stepfather she hated so much. He wondered whether she'd have told him all this if he'd succeeded in getting her to talk or whether she'd have kept some of it to herself. After pressing for answers, he was starting to feel as though he were finally getting somewhere. It was just odd that it was coming from the pages of a diary rather than from Sarah herself. She'd probably be mortified if she knew. And that was another strange thing. The contrast between her then and now was so apparent. Sharing her experiences with Claire, going out of her way to lie to her parents, embracing her rebellious streak. Why had she changed? Why had she clammed up to the point where she never even spoke *to* her family, let alone talked *about* them?

He flicked through the remaining pages of the diary. Undying love for Richard and sexual awakening seemed to be the overwhelming content behind Sarah's neat, joined-up writing. He didn't want to read it. He'd already stepped over a line when he'd opened the first page of her diaries. He didn't need to know about the ins and outs of her sex life with Richard as well. There were some things he was better off not knowing.

18.

27 October

Oh God. This cannot be happening. I feel sick. Like I could throw up and keep going until I puke myself to death. Someone *please* tell me what I'm supposed to do now? This is the worst thing that could possibly happen.

A baby. Shit!

So much for not writing it down in order not to jinx myself. I knew as soon as I told Claire that it would become real. That I'd have to do a test instead of simply pretending my period had forgotten to show up because I've been so stressed out. Maybe that's why I told her, because we both know what happens when you let something like that brew until it's too late. I just didn't want to believe it could be true. Never mind that Adam and I are over or that I'm skint or that soon I won't have anywhere to live. I just can't do this. I can't be pregnant. Not again.

The stupid thing is that I don't even have any symptoms. No morning sickness, no swollen boobs – nothing. And I know you don't need to show symptoms for it to be true, but still. I don't want to believe it. I can't believe it. There can't be a tiny mass of cells multiplying inside of me. There just can't be.

Pregnant. The test said it, as clear as day. None of this 'one line for negative, two lines for positive' crap. There's no getting away from it – it literally spelled it out. P R E G N A N T. Like a slap in the face. I was waiting for the 'not' to pop up in the window, like it was some kind of sick joke. I was convinced it was faulty. It wasn't. The second test in the pack showed the same result, and the other four tests I've taken since. And to make it even more messed up, Adam came home right after I'd taken the last one. I had to hide in the bathroom until the panic began to subside.

I can't cope with this. There's just no way.

What's wrong with me? Why did my bloody stupid egg accept his over-eager sperm? I take the pill every single day, first thing in the morning. I never miss one. Ever. Sure, it's only 99 per cent effective, but did I really have to end up in the 1 per cent? It's not fair.

I wish I didn't feel like this. I wish I could be happy about having a baby with him, but I'm not. I'm scared stiff, and I don't want this baby. I don't deserve it. More than that, I'm doing it a favour. I know it sounds heartless, but it's true. It's taken years for me to feel even remotely normal again.

I can't go through all of that a second time.

19.

Adam looked at the diaries in the box. He'd only just scratched the surface, but he was determined to find out the secret Sarah had been hiding all this time. When he read her diaries, it was almost as if he could hear her voice, like she was sitting next to him, narrating them. He could picture her face, mirroring the emotions she wrote about. It was like he'd been living with a two-dimensional version of her, and now she was becoming a real, full person. Once she opened up, the Sarah he knew was quietly confident, but her fourteen-year-old self? She had been completely different. He could almost feel her effervescence leaping from the page with every word he read. She was rebellious, wily and carefree. What had happened between then and now?

It was a strange way to get to know your girlfriend, but it was a means to an end. He shook his head. *Ex*-girlfriend. Whatever. It didn't matter. The anticipation he felt when he picked the diaries up in his hand – it was exactly the same as he'd felt when they first got together, when she'd walk up to him outside a Tube station or in a bar. He was getting to know her. He couldn't stop now.

∽

TOGETHER APART

Wow, I haven't written anything for ages! I don't know where the time's gone. Well, actually I do. I've been spending it with Richard. We're totally inseparable now, and we meet every day after school before going to his house. It's a bloody pain in the arse because it takes forever to get there, but it's so worth it. We have so much fun together, listening to music, talking and going for walks in the Peak District. I can't believe that. Me, in hiking boots. But it's really beautiful and romantic, and even though his parents are cool with me spending time there, it's nice to be by ourselves.

I can't believe how lucky I am. You hear about girls who lose their virginity and then get dumped straight away. Not me. I've avoided all that, and I'm convinced it's because I waited until he came along instead of settling for someone else. Richard makes me smile so much my face hurts. I'm deliriously happy, and he totally takes my mind off the crap going on at home.

Peter is in a permanent rage with me. Still. I mean, really? Get over it already. I don't care, anyway. I promised myself that I would start doing what I wanted, and that's exactly what I've been doing. He tried grounding me again, but it hasn't worked. I stay out after school, and I come home whenever I feel like it, whether I'm grounded or not. He took my keys off me about a week ago. I actually couldn't believe Mum let him do that. She just let him snatch them off me. Whatever. I'm not bothered. I don't need a key to get in. That's what windows are for.

I've started skipping the last lesson so I can take the bus into town because he's started coming to school to pick me up. It's great. He's livid when I get home late at night because, for all the things he does to try and stop me from going out, I've found ways to outsmart him, and he clearly doesn't like it – not one little bit.

I don't meet Richard at City Hall anymore. Peter figured out
that it was where my friends hung out, and he started showing up
there too, like a mental stalker. He just wouldn't leave me alone.
I think he's got the message now, though. We had a huge argument
yesterday because I stayed overnight at Richard's without asking
him first. I told Claire what I was doing, and she said she would
tell Mum. She's pissing me off by letting Peter do what he wants,
but she's still my mum. I didn't want her to be worried about me.
I'm not *that* irresponsible. Peter was just annoyed because I hadn't
told him. He's a control freak. He has to be in charge of absolutely
everything. He decides what we eat for dinner, what's watched
on the television, even who uses the bloody bathroom first in the
mornings.

I told him what I thought about him last night. I told him that
he wasn't my dad and never would be. I also said that I would never
do anything he told me to, and as far as I was concerned, he didn't
exist. He didn't like that at all. He threatened to chuck me out, but
for once, Mum stepped in. It's the first time she's ever stood up to
him – at least in front of me.

Things have also got much better with me and Claire. It's crazy
to think that just a few months ago, I couldn't wait to have a room
of my own. For ages, all I wanted was my own space and distance
from her, but now I wish we still shared a room. We stay up late
chatting and stuff. She's slept in my bed a few times, and I've slept
in hers. It's funny. She's always been here, but it's only now that
we've got our own rooms that I've realised how much I like having
her around.

24 December 1998

Somehow, I don't think tomorrow's going to be a day to remember.
There are no presents under the tree for me this year. Peter's taking

Mum to Israel next year for her Christmas gift. I think a part of me didn't really believe that he was being serious when he suggested it, but it seems I was wrong. Claire opted out, and he didn't even ask me if I wanted to go. He said it's a treat and my 'behaviour' wasn't deserving of a holiday. Big deal! I'd rather eat glass than go on some lame trip. Mum's best friend is going to keep an eye on us. She only lives a couple of doors up. It's just a shame I have to wait until next year for them to go!

I can't believe he would be so stupid, leaving two teenage girls on their own for a week. If he really thinks we're going to just go to school and come home again every day, he's in for a bloody shock. We're going to have the party to end all parties. For once, we'll be the cool ones. And it means I'll be able to spend a whole week with Richard. How great is that? I know it's ages away yet, but we'll still be together; I know that for sure.

I hope he likes his present. I couldn't really afford anything much since Peter's totally stopped my pocket money, so Claire lent me some. I found a nice silver tobacco tin in a second-hand shop in town. It didn't cost much, but it looks pretty old and valuable. I wonder what he got me.

25 December 1998

Christmas Day. What a load of crap. Mum and that dickhead Peter spent the morning at church, leaving me and Claire alone to sort out our breakfast. There were no presents for me – at least not from them. Surprise, surprise. Peter holds the purse strings, as Mum stopped working when they got married, so he's the only one with any money coming in.

Claire got matching necklaces for me and her with heart-shaped pendants on them, which was nice. We used to get each other things like bath salts, and it was all very impersonal. It's annoying that now we've got close again, I can't afford to get her anything half decent.

I miss Richard. I bet his Christmases are full of fun and laughter, like Christmas should be. They used to be like that when Dad was alive. Me and Claire went to visit his grave this morning. Mum doesn't come with us anymore, but I know she still goes up there. There are always fresh flowers on his headstone. If only he were here now. I bloody hate Christmas.

26 December 1998

I feel sick. Something's going on, I know it. Richard cancelled on me this morning. We were meant to spend the day together, but he phoned and said he wasn't feeling well, so we'd see each other on New Year's Eve instead. That's a whole five days away! I don't understand why he wants to leave it that long. How can he wait that long? It's not like we can't meet up tomorrow or something. I'm going crazy over here. I miss him so much. I hope he's not going off me!

28 December 1998

I saw Daniel in town today. It was really weird. He asked if I've spoken to Richard. Why would he ask that? It was like he knew something I didn't, and now I feel really paranoid. I asked if he'd spoken to him, but he didn't say anything. I know something's wrong. Richard hasn't been to town, and he's always in the shower or something whenever I call him. I don't know what I've done to make him go off me like he has, and I *know* he has. It's obvious he's avoiding me, and I don't know why! What have I done wrong?

31 December 1998

I actually spoke to him today, which was a miracle because I thought he'd dropped off the face of the earth since Christmas Eve. He called like nothing had even happened and asked if I was going to Corp tonight. I said no because firstly, I have no money at all, and second, it's ticket only, and I haven't got one. He said I could go to his instead because his parents would be out at some fancy ball, and I really wanted to tell him to stuff it. I love him and everything, but I didn't want him to think he could just ignore me for ages and then come back whenever he felt like it. But I couldn't. Just hearing his voice again made me melt.

1 January 1999, 4.30 a.m.

Happy Fucking New Year. I want to curl up and die. There's just no bloody point to anything – not when it all turns to shit.

Richard's leaving. His dad's got a new job in New York, and he starts at the end of February. That's two months away. He said he'd known it might be happening for a while but didn't want to say anything in case it never did. It was confirmed on Boxing Day. What a great bloody gift that is.

I was really happy this morning. I mean, I was still annoyed at him, but I hadn't seen him for ages, and really, there was no point in being pissed off about something so small. I was really excited to see him.

We had sex when I got there, and it was amazing. It felt so special, and I nearly cried afterwards because I was so relieved that we were still together, and all my worrying had just been paranoia. I thought the time was right to tell him that I loved him, even if he didn't say it back. I was like a volcano waiting to erupt – I couldn't hold it in anymore, so I said it, and as soon as I did, everything changed.

Seriously, as soon as those words were out of my mouth, he got out of the bed, pulled on his jeans and started rolling a spliff. I thought he was going to tell me he didn't love me back, and I swear to God, my heart was pounding so hard I thought it would crack my ribs right open. That's when he told me. He just mentioned it as if he was talking about the weather.

'We're moving to America,' he said, and my world fell apart.

He said the reason he hadn't wanted to see me until now was because he didn't know how to tell me. He said that he doesn't want to go, but he has no choice, and if he could, he would stay here because he loves me too.

He said it. It was exactly what I'd wanted to hear, but it didn't make me feel happy like I hoped it would because it doesn't fucking matter if he loves me. In a couple of months' time, he won't be here. He'll be thousands of miles away.

Right now, I'm sitting on the floor in his room. He's asleep in bed, and I feel so alone. Everything was going so well, and now it's been ripped to shreds. I'm trying not to cry because if I do, I don't think I'll be able to stop.

20.

9 January 1999

Sometimes, I wonder if I imagined Richard telling me he's leaving. He hasn't said anything about it since New Year's Eve, and it's almost like it never happened. Of course, it did. The fact that everything between us is way more intense now proves it. It's like knowing that he's leaving has made it all seem so much more important. I'm happy when I'm with him, but I really wish the days would stop going by so quickly, because every morning I wake up is a step closer to the day he leaves.

18 January 1999

It's the anniversary of Dad's death soon, and Mum's completely wrecked. She always gets like this. When I got back from Richard's after school, she was slumped on the kitchen table next to an empty bottle of wine. She hadn't made any dinner, and obviously she wasn't in any kind of fit state to be able to. Peter wasn't home, so I went to find Claire, trying not to cry because I really don't like to see Mum like that. Claire's so practical. She found some money in Mum's purse, called us a pizza and then tried to persuade her to go to bed. The whole time, I was praying that Peter wouldn't come home. I didn't want him to walk in and see her like that because he hates drinking, and he'd have gone berserk. I bet he wouldn't even care about why she was in such a state.

In the end, we had to put her arms around our shoulders and try and carry her up the stairs, but she was swaying all over the place. It was like holding up a dizzy elephant, and the smell of the wine on her breath made the back of my throat tingle. We finally made it to her room, and she fell on the bed, passed out. She's fast asleep now, and Peter's downstairs watching TV. We didn't tell him what happened, but I'm pretty sure he could guess. There's no way he could have missed the smell of alcohol when he went into their room.

Poor Mum.

20 January 1999

Peter's thrown away every last drop of wine in the house. I must admit, I expected him to have a go at Mum for getting so drunk, but he hasn't so far. She didn't leave her room all day yesterday, and now he's called a family meeting. I say 'called', but all he's done is stick a note on the fridge.

I wish I could go with Richard and get away from all this. He keeps promising he'll stay in touch, and we'll still go out with each other. He reckons he'll be visiting all the time anyway, to see his grandparents, but I felt like I was going crazy when I didn't see him over Christmas, and that was only for a few days. How the hell will I cope with not seeing him for months at a time?

The thing is, I know I could wait for him. I just don't know if he could wait for me. I know he loves me. He tells me every day. It's just that he'll be surrounded by all these cool American girls. He's hardly going to hold out for little old me, is he?

26 January 1999

We went to the cemetery today to lay some flowers on Dad's grave. It still feels like it was only yesterday. I hate how quickly time goes sometimes. I really wish he could come back for just one day, or even an hour. I just want him to hug me and tell me everything will be okay. Everything would be so much better if he were still here. He was the best dad in the world. I love him so much.

I miss you, Dad.

1 February 1999

We had the family meeting earlier. It was a bit heavier than I was expecting. Apparently, there's to be no more alcohol in the house because Mum's finding it hard to resist the temptation, and she needs to concentrate on living the virtues of Jesus. What a load of crap! Peter's so bloody weird. Why can't he just say the truth instead of preaching all the time? It's obvious – she's an alcoholic. I don't know why he can't just say it as it is instead of being so bloody dramatic.

Mum didn't say anything. I think she felt embarrassed. He was talking about her like she wasn't even there, and really, she might as well not have been. Sometimes I wonder if she has a voice at all. I really don't know why she married him. There's nothing appealing about him at all. When I get married, I want to be head over heels in love. I want to be able to imagine myself growing old with my husband and having lots of kids. I want it to be with someone like Richard.

We still have a few weeks left until he goes, but he's changed. He's less cuddly, and he's more distracted. I think he's trying to put some distance between us. We still spend time together, but it's like his head's somewhere else. I thought I'd have him right up until the day he left, but now I think he's trying to finish it before he goes.

I understand why. Really, I do. But I don't want it to happen. Not right now. I'm so happy with him. He has no idea how much I love him. I can't put it into words. I don't know what I'm going to do without him.

21.

Adam stepped out of the lift and looked at the sign in front of him. What was it that made hospitals smell so bad? Did they pump something through the air vents? Along with the squeaky floors and bright lighting, they were depressing places, full of death and cancer . . . and strokes. His mum's voice had faltered when she'd said that word, and the words on the report he'd been typing at the time jumbled together, swimming in front of his eyes. He'd left the office and raced to the hospital, trying not to think the worst.

He turned left and frowned as he walked down the corridor. What was that film he'd watched years ago? *The Diving Bell and the Butterfly.* That was it. Snippets of it came back to him. The stroke victim, lying in his hospitable bed, completely paralysed and unable to speak, eat – do anything. His dad had just had one of those.

He loosened his tie and shook his arms out. His mum was sitting on a plastic chair up ahead. He couldn't show any fear.

'You're here.' She smiled up at him, and he swallowed the lump in his throat. The relief on her face was palpable.

He sat down and hugged her, suddenly aware of how small she was. 'Where is he?'

She linked her arm through his. 'Having some more tests.'

'What happened?'

'I don't know.' She shook her head slowly. 'We were sitting on the sofa, talking about Christmas and whether to have turkey or goose, and he said his arm felt funny, like he had pins and needles. And then he started slurring. I remembered that advert off the telly about the signs of a . . . you know.'

Adam nodded, rubbing his hand over hers. She must have been terrified. 'I'm sure he's fine.'

'We're not young anymore, Adam. This is it. This is where it all starts.'

'Don't talk like that. He'll be absolutely fine. Let's just wait to see what the doctor says.'

He hoped he sounded confident and strong. The last thing he wanted was for her to worry even more. It was all well and good to tell her to wait for the diagnosis, but all he could think about now was that bloody film. His mum squeezed his arm as a doctor walked through the double doors, but he carried on straight past them.

'Where are Joe and David?'

'Joe's driving down, and David's away somewhere. Some kind of business trip.' She shook her head as a tear rolled down her cheek. 'What if we can't reach him? John might—'

'He won't,' Adam interrupted and put his arm around her. She smelled of Chanel No. 5. It was the only perfume she ever wore, and it had been a staple Christmas and birthday present for as long as he could remember. He shuffled in the hard plastic chair. His dad would be fine. He had to be.

❧

Adam watched as the doctor shone a light into his dad's eyes.

'How are you feeling now, Mr Thompson?' the doctor asked.

'Fine. As right as rain,' John replied.

'Good.' The doctor nodded and put his light back in his jacket pocket. 'You suffered what's called a TIA – a transient ischemic attack. It's caused by a disruption of blood flowing to the brain, and because of that, it's sometimes referred to as a mini-stroke.'

Adam swallowed as his mum's hand flew to her mouth.

'So it *was* a stroke?' Joe asked.

'Not exactly. The symptoms are very similar, but with strokes they're usually permanent, and as I'm sure you're aware, they can be very severe or even fatal. With a TIA the symptoms are short-lived, generally going within twenty-four hours with no lasting tissue damage.'

'So he's going to be okay?' Angela asked, reaching out to hold John's hand.

'He will recover, yes.' He looked at John. 'Your symptoms are all but gone, but you will need to be admitted for further monitoring, and following that, you'll need to make some lifestyle changes.'

'What kind of lifestyle changes?' John asked, and despite their surroundings, Adam stifled a smile. His dad had reacted as if the doctor had suggested he run up and down the ward naked. 'You just said I'll be fine.'

'And you will be. But a TIA is a significant risk factor for stroke, and studies have shown that one in ten people do go on to suffer a stroke within a year if untreated.' The doctor looked down at the clipboard in his hands. 'Your blood pressure is higher than we'd like, and you have high cholesterol. In order to mitigate any further risks, I'd advise a change in diet – more fruits and vegetables – that kind of thing – and regular exercise. It's nothing insurmountable, and you'd be surprised how small changes can go a long way.'

As the doctor carried on, Adam's thumbs sped across his mobile phone to write a text message, and the first name he went to in his address book was Sarah's. It was only when he saw her name on the screen that he realised what he was about to do. It was an automatic response to tell her something so huge, and whilst he knew she'd be supportive, he also knew it was a bad idea. He had to break the need for intimacy with her completely. Instead, he sent the message to David. It was their dad in hospital, after all. For the first time, the concept of his parents, the backbone of his family unit, not being there was a reality. Sarah's dad had died, and she'd estranged herself from her mum. Adam shook his head at the thought. He would never understand it, and he realised that he never wanted to.

∾

The next day, Adam stood under the shower spray and shook his head. Being in the hospital all evening had tired him out, and to say he felt groggy was an understatement. When Joe had texted to say their dad had been discharged, a load had been lifted from his shoulders. There'd be none of his mum's legendary Victoria sponge cake and custard with Sunday dinners now, but it was a small price to pay for the health of his parents.

Adam turned the hot water tap down, bracing himself for the jet of ice-cold water, and forced himself to stand under it. The water pelted his skin like frozen bullets, and after a few seconds, he stepped out and wrapped himself in his towel, warm from being hung on the radiator. He had to get his head out of the world of strokes and teenage diaries, and an afternoon watching football at Carl's would do it.

His head jerked up at the banging noises coming from the hall-way. He swung open the bathroom door to see Sarah throwing bags and boxes from the storage cupboard onto the floor. Water dripped from his hair onto the laminate floorboards.

'What are you doing?'

She ignored him and continued to search frantically through one of the boxes before pushing it to one side.

'Sarah?'

'I need to find something. It's a box of old books of mine – have you seen it?' she asked without looking up.

Shit. He swallowed as goose bumps peppered his skin. She knew he had her diaries. Why else would she be so interested in getting them now? They'd been in the cupboard, undisturbed for months.

'Well, have you seen it? It's really important. I need it.' She stopped rummaging and looked up at him. Her voice sounded weird. He didn't like it.

'I was looking in there for something a couple of weeks ago, and I didn't see anything. If it's there, it must be right at the back.' He clenched his jaw, ignoring the way his head was screaming *lying scumbag* at him. 'Look, it's really dusty in there, and some of that stuff's pretty heavy. Why don't you make us a cup of tea or something, and I'll look for it.'

She looked back towards the cupboard, and he gripped his towel. She needed to go. He had to put the diaries back.

'Okay.' She nodded and got to her feet, pulling the sleeves of her sweater down. 'It's a red and blue shoebox.'

She hovered next to the cupboard door before leaving him in the hallway. He waited until he heard her fill the kettle, before going to his room and pulling on some jeans and a T-shirt. The cotton stuck to his back. He'd come close to getting found out, and after seeing her frantically searching for them, he realised just how important they were to her. He had no right to invade her privacy the way he had.

He carried the box of diaries from his room into the hallway and put them on the floor before pulling on his coat and heading into the kitchen. Sarah was leaning against the worktop staring straight ahead.

'I've found it. It's in the hallway. And don't worry about the tea, I've got to go out anyway.' Adam looked at her, but she said nothing back. 'Right, well, I'll see you later then.'

He left the flat and stepped out onto the street, sucking in a deep breath. That was all way too close, and the way she looked had freaked him out. He'd thought about mentioning his dad's TIA, but it was obvious she wouldn't have even registered his words if he had. He glanced down at his watch. If he left now, he might just catch kick-off. He looked up at the window to their living room. She probably wouldn't tell him what was wrong with her anyway, and now she had her diaries, he was right back to where he'd started.

He climbed into the car and set off for Carl's house. After TIAs and secret diaries, his mind was in a haze, and Sarah was the least of his worries.

22.

I can't believe it. He's dead. Richard is dead.

I thought it was a joke at first. I haven't been able to stop thinking about him the last few days, and it had been so long since I'd last logged into my Facebook account that I'd forgotten my password. I never even wanted to join Facebook. What was the point? I didn't want to reconnect with people from my past. It would defeat the point of trying to put it all behind me, but Claire had insisted and set it up for me. I wanted to see if I could find him on there, but it seemed he'd found me first. My stomach dropped when I saw the message he'd sent – asking if it was really me. I don't have a profile photo, so I guess he didn't know for sure. He'd sent it last spring, and there was only one. Maybe he thought I was ignoring him and gave up, or thought he'd got the wrong Sarah Collins and messaged someone else with the same name.

Just seeing his picture brought back memories of the times we'd spent in his room, kissing and listening to music. He looked good. All dishevelled, with scruffy, long hair and stubble. I wanted to know if he was married or had kids, so I went to his page, but it was obvious that something wasn't right.

There were no status updates from him at all, but people had written on his page, and a lot of them were wishing him a happy birthday. There were messages from Tom, Hannah, Daniel, Frank – it was like being a kid again. Only, they weren't normal. They were all worded wrong, and it was the one from Tom that nearly knocked the wind out of me. *Gone, but never forgotten.*

Still, I tried to tell myself it wasn't true. He'd gone somewhere, emigrated maybe. There was no way it could be anything more serious. And then I saw it. The post from his sister that confirmed everything. The one that said there'd be a memorial service next month. The one that mentioned his headstone being placed.

I had to reread it, and for a second I thought that I was looking at the wrong profile page. But it said quite clearly: Richard Stone. And while there might be millions of Richard Stones in the world, there could only be one who looked like him, and only one who'd message me. I looked through the pictures on his page, and all I could think was that it had to be some kind of sick joke. The mahogany casket, the mountains of flowers and hordes of people stood around his graveside. It couldn't be real.

He messaged me. After years and years, he reached out, doing what I'd never dared to, and now he's dead, his life over. I needed to know how he died because the words 'Richard Stone' and 'dead' just didn't belong in the same sentence. So I looked on *The Star* website and typed his name into the search box. I really didn't expect anything to load other than an obituary page, because even though it didn't make sense to me, I knew, deep down, that this wasn't an elaborate prank. The headline that loaded up was *Local man stabbed to death in revenge attack.*

He'd been stabbed. Eight months ago. He was such a nice guy, the thought of anyone murdering him is inconceivable to me. And for revenge? He'd reported some kids for stealing from his shop, and two days later, he'd been killed. He died protecting his livelihood. It had been recorded on CCTV, and two sixteen-year-olds had been caught, but couldn't be named for 'legal reasons'.

In the years I've been a social worker, I've numbed myself to the awful things I hear on a daily basis. I had a case once where a thirteen-year-old boy was sent to Feltham Prison. He'd been in a gang, and they'd stabbed a passer-by because they were bored. It was horrible, of course, but it didn't get to me. I was removed from it. You hear about things like that all the time on the news, but it didn't happen to people I knew. Until now.

I needed to see his picture. Not the one on Facebook, but the one I took years ago. I wanted to see his face as I remembered it, when we were spending our last few weeks together before he moved thousands of miles away, never to be seen again. I needed my diaries.

Thank God Adam was here. I couldn't find them, and I was getting so frustrated that it would only have been a matter of time before I completely exploded. He found them in no time, and thankfully he left straight away. The relief at him finding the diaries turned pretty quickly into frustration – I just needed him out of there. I'd tried for so long to keep my past and present separate, but now they're intertwining, and I have no idea what to do. Is it really a coincidence that I find out I'm pregnant, and a moment later I find out that Richard is dead? Is it some kind of sick, twisted joke? I've even found myself wondering whether any of this would have happened had I just accepted his proposal and gone on blindly ahead; whether it's some kind of karmic payback.

Why? Why didn't Richard just let the kids go? Why did he have to own a shop instead of working somewhere else? Why did he come back? He might still be alive if he were still in the States.

Why did he have to leave in the first place?

I'd always told myself that I'd speak to him again one day. I just needed to find the courage first. It never occurred to me that I'd never get the chance to. Now, he'll never know.

I've messaged Claire. It was an SOS. I need her here with me. I know this could seriously mess everything up if Adam comes back while she's still here, but right now I really don't care.

I need my sister.

∿

Adam swore at the TV. The match was sixty minutes in, no goals had been scored and now a yellow card was being handed out for a nonexistent tackle.

'That ref needs his eyes tested,' Adam said as Carl returned from the kitchen with two bottles of Coke. 'I don't know why I bother sometimes. It's ninety minutes of my life I won't get back. The least they could do is fucking score.'

Carl raised his eyebrows. 'What's up with you? More dramas with Sarah?'

Adam took a sip of his Coke. He couldn't get the image of Sarah hunting for her diaries out of his head, but he didn't want to talk about it. He felt like scum enough as it was.

'Nothing. Well, my dad had a mini-stroke yesterday, but apart from that it's all fine and dandy.'

'Shit. Is he okay?'

'Yeah, he'll be fine. It could have been a lot worse. The doctor said it was like a warning, really. Still a shock, though.'

Carl nodded. 'I bet.'

From the moment his mum had called with the news, Adam had tried to keep a sense of optimism, refusing to really think about what would have happened had the diagnosis been worse. He'd kept strong for his mum and silent about it with Sarah, but sitting with Carl, who knew his dad as well as if he were his own, a shiver ran down his back as he remembered the way his dad had looked, laid up in the hospital bed. Adam quickly shook his head to dislodge the image.

'What's going on with you anyway? Your smug face is crying out for a punch.'

'Smug? Me?'

'Yes, you. You've been sat there with a stupid grin on your face all afternoon.'

'Nothing. It's just been an interesting few days, that's all.'

'Oh yeah?'

Carl nodded. 'Yeah.'

'So?' Adam gestured for him to elaborate.

'Jeez, what is this? The Spanish Inquisition?'

'Who is she?' Adam laughed.

Carl shook his head. 'Is it that obvious?'

'Call it a lucky guess.'

'Just a customer from work. She dropped her car in for a service, and we got talking. I'm taking her out on Tuesday,' Carl said with a shrug.

'What, like on a date?'

'Yeah. I have been on dates before, you know. Besides, being casual all the time's getting a bit boring.'

Adam spluttered into his bottle. 'Are you feeling all right?'

'It had to happen sometime. I won't be young forever.'

'Since when has that ever bothered you?'

'Since you ended up a sad diary reader after we all thought you were going to sail off into the sunset and live happily ever after.'

'Cheers, mate.' Adam winced. 'Don't sugar-coat anything, will you?'

'I'm just saying, life's too short to screw around.'

'You're the one who's been telling me to get back out there. "Plenty more fish in the sea" and all that crap, remember? Now you're saying we're too old?'

'I know what I said, but you seemed so messed up, I had to tell you something. And it got me thinking. Sarah walked all over you, and yet you still want her back.' Carl shook his head. 'That's pretty special. I've never had that. I've never let a woman get close enough to do that, and you know me: I never like to miss out.'

Adam nodded. It was true. Carl had to have everything everyone else had, if not better. It must have been something to do with being the younger brother.

'So while we're talking about romance, how are you feeling about Jen and Nick?'

Carl grimaced. 'Don't. Just thinking about it makes me feel ill.'

'She asked me to talk to you. I don't think she's joking about how she feels.'

'I know she isn't.' Carl shrugged. 'I just don't want to get involved, and I know that at some stage, I will.'

Adam smiled. 'You'll be her brother-in-law before you can even blink.'

'Don't.'

'Seriously, though. Are you really that against it?'

'I dunno.' Carl sighed. 'Nick reckons he's really into her, but . . .'

'You don't trust him.'

'It's not a matter of trusting him. It's just that I know him. He's had girls he's been serious about before, but this is different. I don't want to have to pick sides if it goes belly up.'

Adam nodded. It was a fair argument, but he knew Carl would come round eventually. He might not like what was going on, but he wouldn't be the one to stand in the way of his brother and best friend being happy. Adam had spoken to him about it, like he'd promised Jenny he would, but that was as far as he was going to go.

'So, this girl,' Adam said. 'Where are you taking her?'

'Some little cocktail place near Goodge Street. Dinner, maybe.'

What was that look in his eye? Wistful? Christ, he'd never used that word before in his life, but that's what it was, and coupled with the fact that Carl was actually taking this woman on a date, it spelled out how serious it could become.

'Yes, yes, go on!' Carl thumped his fist on the arm of the sofa, and Adam turned his attention to the television just in time to see the ball hit the back of the net.

Carl clinked his bottle against Adam's. There would be no more mushy talk.

⚬

As Adam closed the front door of the flat behind him, he heard the sound of a cupboard closing in the kitchen and recalled Sarah's hunt for her diaries earlier. What had happened to make her need them again so badly? He wandered in to see her bending down in front of the oven, peering through the glass at whatever she was cooking in there. It smelled like chicken.

But something was different, and it took a second to realise that her hair was straight. Her gorgeous curls were gone. Why? He was just about to speak when she spun around. There was no doubt about it – it wasn't her. The face was the same, but there was makeup on it. Sarah didn't wear makeup.

'You must be Adam.'

'Claire?'

23.

Damn. He wasn't supposed to know about her. He clenched his jaw and looked at her. This was beyond weird.

'Hi.' He awkwardly shook her outstretched hand. How was he supposed to greet his ex-girlfriend's previously nonexistent twin, exactly?

'I hope you don't mind me taking over your kitchen?' Claire asked, nodding towards the cooker.

'No, not at all. Help yourself.' He opened a cupboard and took out a glass.

'It's nice to meet you finally. Although it would've been nicer under different circumstances.'

What circumstances? He nodded in agreement, bluffing out the fact that he didn't have the first idea about what she was referring to.

'Yeah. You too. Where's Sarah?'

'Sleeping. She was pretty upset. I think she finally tired herself out.'

'How's she doing?'

This was a delicate situation. He had to be careful about what he said. The wrong thing could send the precarious house of cards built around them crashing down.

Claire frowned. 'She's just found out her childhood sweetheart's been murdered; how do you think she's doing?'

'What?' Adam raised his eyebrows.

'She *has* spoken to you about everything, hasn't she?' Claire squinted her eyes at him.

Should he lie or tell the truth? Sarah might have told Claire that she'd never mentioned she was a twin, but then again, for all Claire knew, he might have known about her all along. After all, she didn't react when he automatically knew it was her crouching in front of the cooker, and not Sarah.

'Of course she hasn't,' Claire said to herself, folding her arms and shaking her head. 'This is Sarah we're talking about, after all. You don't know anything, do you?'

Adam shrugged and sat at the table. He couldn't lie to her. It was unnerving him enough having a carbon copy of Sarah in front of him.

'Maybe I shouldn't be so hard on her.' Claire sighed and sat on the chair opposite him. 'At least she told you about me. Believe me, that's progress.'

He swallowed with relief. He hadn't needed to lie. She'd jumped to her own conclusions, and he was happy to go along with it. It was a better option than admitting that Sarah hadn't told him anything, and he only knew who she was because he'd poked his nose into Sarah's private teenage diaries.

'So, what's all this about a murder?'

'Apparently he was stabbed. Did you want a drink?' Claire asked, nodding at the empty glass in his hand. He'd been so distracted he'd forgotten he was even holding it.

'Yeah, silly me. Did you want one?'

'I'd love a glass of wine if you have any.'

'How did she find out?'

'Facebook. It happened a while ago, but she doesn't keep in touch with anyone back home these days. It was pure chance that she found out at all, really.'

'That's awful. I'm sorry,' Adam said, returning to the table with a bottle of Chablis.

Claire shrugged. 'I never met him. All I know about him is what Sarah told me. But yeah, it's sad. And it's hit her really hard.'

Adam frowned as he poured out the wine. 'I don't want to seem insensitive or anything, but I don't get why this has got to her so badly. I mean, when's the last time she saw him?'

'Oh God.' Claire puffed her cheeks out. 'Years ago. When we were still at school.'

'When I left this afternoon, she was really out of it, and then I come back to find her knocked out and you in my kitchen.'

Claire played with the stem of her wine glass. 'I wish I could tell you everything. Honestly, I do. I've heard a lot about you, and you seem like a great guy, but it's not my place to tell you. You have to ask her.'

Adam looked at her. Clearly she knew about Sarah's secret.

'Has it got something to do with why we've split up? Because believe me, I've tried to get her to talk, and she won't budge. To be perfectly honest, it's getting a little old.'

Maybe it was the familiarity of her face, but he felt comfortable talking with her, despite the fact that they'd only just met.

'I know.' Claire nodded. 'And even though she'd kill me for saying this, I know she still loves you.'

He gave her a half-hearted smile. He already knew that Sarah still loved him, but it made little difference, and the fact that Claire had tried to persuade Sarah to talk to him only made him feel worse. She was sitting in his kitchen because Sarah needed her. It made sense that if Claire had something to say, Sarah would listen. But she hadn't listened, and that was the problem. If Claire had told her to come clean about her past and whatever it was that was holding her back, she hadn't acted on that advice. Which meant that asking her to open up to him again was pointless. If she wouldn't listen to Claire, her twin sister, then why would she listen to him?

His shoulders sagged. He'd never know the truth. All the sneaking around and reading her diaries had been a complete waste of time. He was no closer to getting any answers today than he had been a week ago, and now that Sarah had her diaries back, he never would be. Claire knew everything and he knew nothing.

'I know what you're thinking,' Claire said as she swirled the wine around in her glass. 'You're thinking that if she hasn't told you by now, then she never will. The thing about Sarah is that she does a mighty fine ostrich impression. She'll bury her head in the sand and try to pretend that everything's okay. It's what she always does; it's just the way she is. But there are things happening that are pushing her to breaking point.'

'Things that, I suppose, you can't tell me?' Adam said with a hint of sarcasm.

'She wouldn't have asked me to come here if things weren't bad,' Claire continued. 'We're not close like that, as much as it kills me to say it. So, I hear you when you say you've tried talking to her and got nowhere, but I know she can't continue like this. Besides, I'm flying back out on Monday, and I don't want to leave her in such a bad way. You two really need to talk.'

'Tell me something I don't know.' Adam took a gulp of wine. 'What do you do? Can't you get compassionate leave or something?' he asked.

'I'm a flight attendant – long haul. Getting cover at such short notice won't be easy, especially since I didn't even know him. I've asked for leave. I just need to wait for cover to be sorted out.'

'So what's it like? Jetting off all over the place?'

'Tiring.' Claire smiled. 'I did short haul for years and switched over a few months ago. It's not bad, and first class is way better than economy.'

'Rubbing shoulders with the rich and famous, huh?'

'Sometimes, though sometimes they're even worse than the stag parties I couldn't wait to get away from.'

Adam watched her as she spoke about her job. She was so different from Sarah. Sarah was so shy that he'd been worried when she first met his friends. It took a couple of meetings for her to loosen up and show them her true personality. He could tell that Claire would be able to walk into a room full of strangers and befriend them all in an instant.

Sarah was so much the opposite of his exes that it was hard to imagine what she would be like if she were the type of girl who had manicures, pedicures and facials. Looking at Claire gave him a fair idea. Everything about her smacked of sophistication. Her honey-coloured hair hung in a perfectly straight sheet down to her shoulders, and her clothes were undoubtedly designer. Even her sweet perfume smelled expensive.

Claire cut her sentence short, turning her head a little as if she were listening for something. Adam concentrated, but aside from the quiet hum of the oven, the flat was quiet. Seconds later, he heard the muffled sound of Sarah crying. Was it some freaky twin thing? How had she heard it before him?

Claire stood up. 'I should go see if she's okay. Would you mind keeping an eye on the chicken?'

'Yeah, sure.'

Claire left him alone in the kitchen, and he rubbed the bridge of his nose. It had been a weird, weird day, but now Claire was here, he felt a glimmer of hope. She seemed like a fixer. Maybe she *could* talk Sarah around.

24.

The next morning, Adam walked into the kitchen to see Claire making coffee, or trying to.

'How does this thing work?' She looked up at him.

'Here, I'll do it.' He took the tub of ground coffee from her.

Talk about déjà vu. When the coffee machine had first been delivered, Sarah had stood in the very same spot and asked the same thing. She never had worked out how to use it. She was a tea drinker anyway.

After she'd left him in the kitchen last night, Claire hadn't come back. He'd heard her leave Sarah's room in the early hours for what would have been an extremely late dinner or early breakfast.

'That's a pretty snazzy machine,' Claire said.

'I'm a bit of a coffee snob, I suppose.' He put a long shot glass under the spout. 'My first job was as a barista. I haven't touched instant since and you won't find any in the cupboards either.'

'I noticed.' Claire grinned back at him. 'I was starting to worry I'd have to drink tea.'

Adam smiled as she pretended to shudder. Claire hated tea and Sarah hated coffee. Claire was already dressed and made up, but if Sarah walked into the kitchen at that exact moment, he would bet she would still be in her pyjamas with bed-hair.

'How is she?' he asked, handing her the glass of coffee.

'She's fine, considering.' Claire took a sip. 'This is a good espresso. I need it after last night.'

'You didn't sleep well? I know the sofa's a bit uncomfortable.'

Claire laughed and shook her head. 'I bunked with Sarah. I'd forgotten how much she snores. I don't know how you managed to cope sleeping next to her for all this time.'

Adam laughed and took his coffee. 'Yeah. She does snore a bit sometimes.'

'It can't have been easy the last couple of months.'

That was an understatement. It had been anything but. It had been frustrating, confusing, annoying, angering and horribly bittersweet.

'Shit happens, right?' Adam replied with a small laugh.

'Yep, it certainly does.'

'So how come you still have an accent and Sarah doesn't?'

'I dunno. Sheffield is definitely in the past for Sarah. She hated the place, but I love it.'

'You two really are different.'

'We had different experiences growing up there.' Claire shrugged. 'It's not really surprising. I had it much easier. I hung around with a more popular set of people and I was a bit more reserved than Sarah.' Claire smiled and shook her head. 'She was a total nightmare back then. Forever grounded.'

Adam raised his eyebrows, even though he already knew about Sarah's rebellion. 'And you?'

'I guess I just dealt with things differently. When Mum remarried after Dad died, I didn't like it but I went along with it. But, Sarah had already changed by then and you know how stubborn she is.'

Adam nodded. 'She's possibly the single most stubborn person I've ever met.'

Claire laughed. 'She was way worse back then and so was Peter, our stepdad. I think it would be fair to say they didn't see eye to eye. I kept out of it for the most part.'

'Are you sure you're actually twins?' Adam smiled.

Claire looked at him and frowned. 'It's funny you say that. If I didn't know any better, I'd say she never even told you about me.'

For a split second, he faltered as he took a sip of his coffee. 'Really? What makes you say that?'

'I don't know.' She shrugged. 'Not that it matters, because obviously she did. I think I'll stay tonight as well.'

'Of course. Do you want my room?'

'No, I'm good. But thanks.'

Her eyes scanned his face like a radar. He was certain she knew that Sarah hadn't told him she was a twin, and he could see the lies starting to unravel right in front of him. How much longer was he going to be able to keep it going?

∽

30 October

Thank God for Claire. I don't think I could have coped without her. I can't even imagine what Adam thought when he met her. I just hope he hasn't judged me too harshly for keeping her a secret.

Having her here felt like the old days when we shared a room. I've been asleep most of the time, but just knowing she's here is like being wrapped in a comfort blanket. It's made the shock of what happened to Richard more bearable. I wish she could stay a little longer, but she has to leave today. It means a lot that she dropped everything and came here for me.

She tried to persuade me to keep the baby. I knew she would, but I'm not going to change my mind, and she respects that, even if she doesn't like it. I know she'll stand by me like she always has. She doesn't like that I'm not going to tell Adam, but she understands why I can't. Even if I could, I don't have the strength to. It's been hard enough to just sit up and write this entry. I know this is all going to get much worse before it gets better.

I'm just so tired.

❧

Adam tried to focus his blurry vision as he showered. For the second night in a row, he'd heard Claire's hushed whispers and Sarah's crying coming from the other side of the wall, and in the end, he'd slept on the sofa. At least Claire was here. Knowing Sarah as he knew her now, there was no way she'd turn to him for support. It made him feel sick to admit it, but it was true. And nobody should have to grieve alone.

He stepped out of the shower and reached for his towel. He swore as it dropped, landing half on the floor and half in the bin. He bent down to pick it up. Thankfully, the bin was empty aside from some cotton pads and a leaflet. Adam looked at his reflection and frowned for a second before going back to the bin and picking up the leaflet. He recognised the brand name on it, and his hands shook as he unfolded the paper, his stomach churning with every movement he made. It was a pregnancy test.

He scanned the words as if it would tell him what the hell was going on. It *could* be Claire's, but the cold shiver running through his body told him it wasn't. It was Sarah's. He'd bet money on it. Was she pregnant? Was the test positive, or was it a false alarm? When did she take it, and why hadn't she told him?

Was the baby someone else's?

He shook away the dizziness that particular thought caused. He refused to think that about her, even with the strange way she'd been acting. If she *was* pregnant, then the baby was his. Maybe that was why she wanted to split up. But that didn't make any sense either. Getting pregnant wasn't any more of a valid excuse to split than the wishy-washy one she'd given him already.

He dropped the leaflet back into the bin and rubbed his hands over his eyes. When would all this drama stop? It was getting to the stage where he could barely remember what his life was like before this whole mess started, and he couldn't see when it would ever end. With the addition of his dad's hospital trip, it was like his life had turned into a skewed soap opera.

Adam rolled his head back and let out a loud sigh before going to get dressed. He was trying to think about anything other than the leaflet he'd found, and it worked until he walked into the kitchen and saw Sarah making a cup of tea. When she heard him behind her, she turned around, and his eyes involuntarily flicked to her stomach, as if he'd be able to tell whether she was carrying his child simply by looking. It wasn't as if he could ask her outright, not now that she was grieving over her dead secondary-school boyfriend.

'How are you feeling?' he asked.

Sarah shrugged. 'I've been better.'

'I was sorry to hear about your friend,' he said as he stuck a glass under the tap.

'Thanks.' She blinked back tears.

What was he supposed to do next? He didn't want to say anything else in case she broke down, but the question of her pregnancy was hanging between them like the elephant in the room. Irritation welled inside of him. He was sick of pussyfooting around her and being unable to ask her anything that really mattered. He was going to give her one last chance and that was all. No matter how much he loved her, he wasn't about to beg. He had more self-respect than that.

'Sarah,' he said, looking her dead in the eye. 'Have you got something you want to tell me?'

Her eyes widened for a second, and it was written all over her face. She knew that he knew about the test. What else would he be referring to? He'd stopped asking why she'd chosen to end their relationship a long time ago. He looked right at her, willing her to tell him something – anything. But she stayed silent, adding to the already tense air in the flat.

Adam counted down from twenty in his head. When he got to zero, he put his glass of water down and walked out. He was done. He'd chased after her, only to be met by her flat rejection, and defended her when his friends had told him he deserved better, but she still wouldn't open up to him. He didn't even feel angry any-more. All he felt as he opened the front door was disappointment.

'Adam, wait.'

He turned and looked at her, keeping his hand on the latch. 'What for? I don't have the energy for this anymore. I've got other things to worry about than you, and if you bothered to stop being so selfish, you'd know that.'

She shook her head. 'I'm not being selfish.'

'When's the last time you asked how I was? My dad had a stroke, but you couldn't possibly know that because everything is all about you. Well, guess what? I'm done.'

'Oh my god. Is he okay? Was it serious? Why didn't you tell me?'

Her eyes were wide, and the colour had drained from her cheeks. She loved his family almost as much as he did – she'd said as much herself. Adam sighed and took his hand off the door latch.

'He's fine. It was a TIA – a mini-stroke.' He shook his head as he spoke. 'It wasn't serious.'

'You should have told me,' Sarah replied softly.

'How? When?' He shrugged his shoulders. 'We don't speak anymore.'

As if to punctuate his point, she didn't reply, and he looked at her and sighed. 'You see? This is exactly what I mean. I can't deal with this shit anymore.'

'What do you want me to say?'

'How about the truth? Why don't you try telling me what's going on with you instead of clamming up all the time?'

Sarah shook her head. 'It's not that easy.'

'You open your mouth and words come out. It's not exactly difficult.'

'I've tried, Adam.'

'Really?' He raised an eyebrow at her and turned to leave the flat. 'Maybe you should try harder.'

25.

Things couldn't get any worse. He knows. I know he does. The way he asked if there was something I needed to tell him was obvious, and when he left, I looked around the flat and realised I'd thrown a leaflet for one of the tests in the bin. I'm so fucking stupid!

I wanted to tell him. I really did. I just couldn't get the words out of my mouth, especially after he told me about his dad. I was so scared for him. I know what it's like to lose a parent, and I'd do anything to protect him from that kind of pain.

Everything is such a mess. He stormed out, and I have no idea where he's gone or when he'll be back, or even *if* he'll be back. I feel sick, and it's not just because of Adam. It's funny how I went without a single symptom, but now that I know I'm pregnant, my body seems to want to ram it in my face from the moment I wake up. At least I haven't actually been sick. I'm trying not to be because if I do, it would be like acknowledging that it exists. Which is ridiculous. I know it does. My appointment at the clinic is tomorrow, and it's not like I'm going for a nice day out. It just makes the whole thing a lot easier if I pretend that this isn't really happening. Not the smartest of moves, I know. I've been here before. Ignoring it won't make it go away.

I wish Claire was still here. I could really use the support tomorrow.

ᕫ

He was supposed to be working, but after almost two hours of being in the office, Adam hadn't even so much as looked at his inbox. For once, there was nothing booked into his diary. He normally craved days like today, and ideally he would be catching up on all the things he never seemed to find the time to do, like the filing or putting together a database for all the maintenance on the apartments. There was an endless list of things he should be doing. Looking on websites to see how his hypothetical child was developing was not one of them.

He couldn't get the niggling curiosity about what might be going on inside her out of his head. His resolve was slipping away, and he found himself giving in to the urge to type into the search bar the words that had been whizzing around in his head all morning.

The results loaded, and he clicked on the first link. He bit the skin on the side of his thumb as he read. Supposing she'd become pregnant at the end of their relationship, she'd be around twelve weeks gone, and he looked at the images on the screen. At twelve weeks old, the baby was two inches long, had fingernails, a tongue and individual fingers and toes. The picture next to the text showed a distinctly human-looking foetus.

A lump formed in his throat, and he closed the browser. He'd read enough.

ᕫ

4 November

Today has been the second worst day of my life. I don't understand how things can keep getting worse. It feels like I'm in the middle of a never-ending nightmare.

The clinic wasn't how I thought it would be. I'd expected a waiting room full of women, quietly dabbing the tears away with crumpled tissues, but after signing myself in with the receptionist, I was surprised to see the waiting room full of women and couples watching TV or flicking through magazines. None of them looked upset or ashamed or disgusted with themselves, and it made me feel awkward because I felt all of those things. I stared at a spot on the wall, trying to ignore the stinging in my eyes as they built up with tears. I didn't want to cry. Not when everyone else seemed so calm in comparison. Even though I knew it was natural to feel how I did, I didn't have the right to cry. Nobody was forcing me to be there. It was a choice I had made myself, albeit with good reason.

It just didn't make sense. I couldn't see how I'd ended up there, in that waiting room, when it was only a few weeks ago that I'd been feeling like the happiest woman on the planet. So I focused on holding back the urge to pee. I'd been told to keep my bladder full in case they needed to do a scan, and the concentration helped, but when they called my name, I thought I'd faint. I had to keep telling myself that it would soon be over.

The nurse sat me down and asked questions about my health and medical history. I told her I was perfectly healthy, no adverse medical history. I lied, telling her my main reason for wanting to terminate was the breakdown of my relationship with Adam. I didn't want to bring a baby up by myself. Apparently, it was a satisfactory answer. I sat in that leather-padded chair, looking at the plastic flowers in a vase and the small silver frame with the picture of her and her partner sitting on a beach, and I didn't waver. I had no doubts – until the scan. It was standard procedure, apparently.

I'd kept my eyes closed until the sonographer squeezed the ice-cold gel onto my stomach. For some unknown reason, I opened my eyes. Maybe it was some kind of sick way of torturing myself, but even up until that point, I still had no doubts. She twiddled some buttons, and the monitor flickered into life, and I wondered how many other women had lain on that bed before me. Thousands, probably. I couldn't help but think of what their circumstances might have been. Were they all like me? Were they in relationships or single? Happy or sad? Relieved or doubtful?

Even now, I don't know why I turned my head towards the monitor when she rubbed the probe thing over my nonexistent bump, but I did, and out of the fuzziness, the image came to life. I wanted to tear my eyes away, but I couldn't. I could see it, and I could hear the sonar-like sound of its heartbeat echoing in the room. It was the loudest thing I'd ever heard in my life. It was so quick and steady that it felt like I was being deafened with it.

The sonographer didn't speak as she took notes, but I saw her eyebrows knitting together, and then she picked up the phone to call in a doctor. Something was clearly wrong, and for a second I thought I'd miscarried. I don't know why I thought that. I'd heard the baby's heartbeat myself, but when the doctor came in and looked at the screen, I still expected to hear that I'd lost it. I wasn't prepared for what he actually said.

I was carrying twins. Or, technically, I *had* been carrying twins. They could only detect one heartbeat, but there was a second foetus that had stopped growing at around eight weeks. The other baby was fine, and they put my pregnancy at a day under thirteen weeks.

I completely lost my voice. I couldn't speak. I could hardly even breathe; my throat had completely closed up. My own heartbeat was pounding in my ears, and my stomach wouldn't stop turning. The idea of one baby was bad enough, let alone two, but knowing that I'd lost one is something I still can't get my head around.

It's like imagining life without Claire. It's simply inconceivable, and even thinking about it gives me a physical ache so bad, it makes me feel like throwing up. I couldn't imagine my life without her in it, no matter how distant we sometimes are.

Until this morning, I thought I was carrying one baby, and terminating that one would have been hard enough. Now it turns out there were two – or had been. One had died and the other lived. The idea of terminating the surviving twin is one I don't know how to deal with. I wish I could tell Adam. Maybe I should. He already knows something's going on. I don't know if I can deal with this on my own, but how do I tell him I'll be aborting his child, especially now that I've lost one of them already?

And if all that wasn't enough, I stopped in at the supermarket on the way home to get some painkillers and bumped into Jenny. She was colder than ice when she saw me, and she told me that Adam had already moved on. She didn't say anything more than that, but it was the *way* she said it. There was no doubt about what she meant. He's slept with someone else. I almost threw up on her shoes when she said that, but what could I say back? That I still love him, and by the way, I'm carrying his child? Hardly. Still, I haven't been able to stop thinking about what she said. I keep picturing him kissing some faceless woman. I have no right to be angry with him, but I am. I'm angry that he's apparently moved on so quickly. It was like she reached into my chest and crumbled my heart into a billion pieces when she told me.

I just want all this to be over.

26.

I think I got about an hour's sleep last night and I really wish I hadn't. I dreamt I was in labour. It was awful. I wasn't in any pain. My whole body felt numb, but I could feel a tugging sensation. It reminded me of when I had my wisdom teeth out, feeling something being ripped from my body.

I was lying on a bed, and my belly was swollen to epic proportions, much more than could ever be possible for a human, and when I looked down, I saw the baby moving. My skin was rippling and stretching as the bulge swarmed around in my belly like an alien trying to burst its way out. A group of midwives were standing around the room with their arms crossed, looking at me like I was the most disgusting thing they'd ever seen – it was etched all over their faces. And standing in the middle of them all was Adam. I was calling out to him, begging him to forgive me, but I couldn't get the words out. The words clogged up in my throat, choking me. The feeling of panic was so real.

Then the baby came. And then another. And another. Baby after baby, after baby. They plopped out of me, blue and lifeless, piling up on the hospital bed. Every single one of them was dead. I don't know how many there were – they just kept coming and coming. Nobody would help me, and eventually Adam and the midwives left the room, leaving me with an ever-growing pile of dead babies. Then one of them turned its head towards me and opened its eyes. They were black. No irises, no nothing. Just endless black holes, and that's when I woke up.

My heart was pounding so much I thought it would leap right out of my chest. I could feel my pulse throbbing in my throat so hard it made me feel sick. My T-shirt was stuck to my body with sweat, like a second skin, and my hair had tangled itself around my neck. I must have been thrashing about pretty badly.

I don't need to be a psychiatrist to know what the dream meant. I know it was the guilt that triggered it. When I came back from the clinic yesterday, I lay on my bed thinking about the twin that had survived. I wondered whether it knew that it was suddenly by itself in there. Whether it felt lonely.

When Adam came back from work, he knocked on the bedroom door, and I pretended to be asleep. I couldn't face him. I didn't move from the bed. I didn't eat. I didn't watch the television. I didn't even text Claire like I'd promised. It was like I was in a trance, and after waking up from that awful nightmare, I lay looking out of the skylight window, watching the night sky become lighter and lighter, until I heard Adam get up for work. I know I have to tell him. He's not stupid. I'm sure he's already guessed the truth, and it wouldn't be fair on him to keep him hanging on. Morally, telling him would be the right thing to do, but I don't want to keep it. And telling him that will kill him, just like it's killing me. The nightmare I had has been playing in my head all day. I'm so sick of carrying this feeling around. I felt it about Richard, and now I'm feeling it about Adam.

❦

It's Richard's memorial on Monday, and after being convinced I didn't want to go, I'm now thinking that maybe I should pay my respects and say goodbye. He was such a huge part of my life, and I can't help feeling that all this is some kind of sign. It has to be more than just coincidence that I found out about Richard's death and my pregnancy in the space of a couple of days. Maybe going will do something to help me move on. All I know is that I have to do something and, if I don't go, I'm not sure I'll ever be able to forgive myself.

27.

Adam diverted Jenny's call. He was the only person left in the office, and if he had any hope in hell of leaving before seven, he needed to concentrate. No doubt she wanted to find out if he'd spoken to Carl about her and Nick. He'd debrief her later.

He sighed and turned his attention back to his computer screen. He frowned, reading the dilapidation report. It wasn't unusual for an apartment to need a few repairs when a tenant vacated, but this was ridiculous. They'd put a hole the size of a basketball in the wall, and the bathroom was dotted with cracked tiles. His mobile rang again, and he groaned in frustration before answering.

'Jen, this really isn't a good time. I've got a ton of work to do – can I call you back later?'

'Oh, good. You're not at home yet.'

'No, I'm still in the office.' He pulled his eyebrows together. 'Why?'

'I think I did something bad.'

'What?' he replied warily.

'I ran into Sarah at the supermarket the other day.'

'Oh great.' No doubt Jenny would have given Sarah a piece of her mind. 'And?'

'I might have let it slip that you pulled when we went out.'

'You did what? For fuck sake, Jenny.'

'I'm sorry. I didn't mean to. I was just so angry with her. It just slipped out.'

'Bullshit.' He turned away from the computer screen. 'Things like that don't just *slip out*. What the hell were you playing at?'

He shook his head. Sure, he was a single man, but with the complications between him and Sarah, this was something that didn't need to be added to the mix – not when she was carrying the baby he desperately wanted her to keep.

'I didn't actually *say* that you had; I just said that you were doing a lot better and you'd moved on.'

'You had no right to say that,' Adam shouted, getting up from his desk. 'You have no idea what you've done.'

'I said I was sorry,' Jenny snapped down the phone.

'No, you're not. You never liked her anyway.'

'That's not true, and you know it.'

He scowled, gripping the phone. 'Just stay out of my business, Jenny.'

He hung up the phone, kicked the filing cabinet and swore to the empty room. Just when it had looked like things couldn't get any worse.

❧

Adam put his key in the lock and sighed. Sarah had been spending more and more time in her room, and now that he'd spoken to Jenny, he understood why. If she was pregnant, then finding out he'd already slept with someone else would hardly have her doing star jumps around the room, whether they were together or not. Jenny was one of his closest friends, and as much as he loved her, he knew what she could be like. She'd been angry at Sarah from the moment Adam had told her about their break-up, and he doubted she'd have given Sarah the news with a coating of sugar.

He frowned as he closed the door behind him. The air was filled with the scent of spices. Lamb tagine. He was certain of it. It was one of Sarah's favourite meals.

He chucked his bag onto his bed before going into the kitchen. The table was laid out with placemats and wine glasses. Had he slipped through a wormhole into a parallel universe?

Sarah was stood by the cooker, spooning a little of the meat into her mouth. After her run-in with Jenny, she was probably about to lace his food with arsenic.

'What's going on?' he asked, removing his tie.

He looked at the kitchen. Sarah was the messiest cook he'd ever seen. Every surface was littered with bowls, kitchen paper and various packets of herbs and spices.

'We need to talk,' she said. The determination in her voice unnerved him. It was something he hadn't heard in a long time. Maybe he was about to get some answers.

∽

As the flavours burst on his tongue, he couldn't help but think back to the first time she had cooked this for him. It was the weekend they'd moved into the flat, and after spending the morning walking around John Lewis picking up rugs and cushions, she'd prepared a Moroccan feast: cinnamon and pumpkin soup, lamb tagine with couscous and spiced vegetables, followed by fruit in ginger syrup with cardamom yoghurt. He'd never tasted anything so good. It had been an idyllic weekend, and back then it felt like anything was possible. If he closed his eyes, he could almost pretend that everything was how it used to be. That they were a normal couple enjoying a nice meal. He could almost believe they were back together. Almost. Why was she being so nice?

Adam swallowed his lamb and looked at her. 'What's this all about, Sarah?'

'I'm pregnant.'

The words fell from her mouth like a bomb falling from a plane, and for a few seconds all he could do was blink. It wasn't entirely a shock, but after the way she'd been so reluctant to tell him anything, hearing her confirm it in such an abrupt way jolted his brain. It was as if he'd found that leaflet in a dream, and now reality hit him sharply in the face. She was pregnant.

'About thirteen weeks I think, give or take.'

He'd been right. She was having a baby. *His* baby. His imagination propelled forwards, and he pictured the two of them in the flat with a screaming baby. His pulse went into overdrive. The thought of dirty nappies, piles of laundry, sleepless nights and the end to his life as he knew it sent a chill through him. Of course he wanted children. He wanted a whole brood of them. Just not right now. And definitely not like this, with a woman who seemed to keep one secret after another.

'I know it's a bit of a shock, but before you start freaking out, you should know that I'm not going to keep it.'

'What do you mean?' His head was reeling – he couldn't keep up with what was going on.

'I'm going to have an abortion.'

He opened his mouth and closed it again. She was going to have an abortion? How could she make a decision like that without even considering him?

'And you didn't think to ask for my opinion?'

'I don't expect you to understand, Adam, but I can't have this baby,' Sarah said. He raised his eyebrows at the strength in her voice.

'What? I mean, I know things are messed up between us, but you know I'd help you raise it. You wouldn't have to do it on your own, regardless of what's going on with us. I'd never do that to you.'

What was he saying? How had his mouth tricked his brain like that? He shook his head again, trying to untangle his thoughts. Only a few seconds ago, he'd been disturbingly close to crapping himself at the idea of becoming a dad. Now he was defending it.

'I know you wouldn't.'

'So think again, then. You don't have to have an abortion, Sarah.'

'Adam, please. This is hard enough as it is,' she said, wiping a tear from her cheek. 'I don't want it, and it's not fair on either of us to keep it, not to mention on the baby itself.'

He looked down at the food on their plates and shook his head. 'You know, that's exactly what you said when we got back from holiday. You said you couldn't be with me anymore because it wasn't fair. Are you ever going to tell me what that was about?'

'This isn't about you. It's about me.'

For a split second, a look passed across her face that told him she was deadly serious. Her usually bright eyes were as dull as dishwater, and she looked like she was about to burst into tears, but he didn't care. This was too big to let go of.

'This whole fucking thing has been about you, Sarah,' he shouted and stood up from the table. 'From the minute you turned me down, everything that's happened has been about you, and now you're telling me that your decision to abort our baby has nothing to do with me. Like my feelings don't count for anything.'

'I needed to figure things out for myself, and you'd have just confused me. I've made my mind up about this, and it has nothing to do with you.'

'It's my baby! Of course it does. How can you be so fucking heartless? You could have talked to me about it. I'd have supported your decision, but you could at least have let me have a say.'

What was wrong with her? He'd really over-estimated her. She clearly wasn't the woman he'd thought she was. His entire body prickled with a fury demanding to be unleashed as he tried with everything he had to contain it. How could she say this wasn't about him? For all she knew, he might have actually supported her decision. He didn't know what he wanted, but she could have at least considered him.

They'd been together for almost a year and lived together for nearly six months. But listening to her now, it looked like she didn't know him at all if she really thought he'd try to convince her to do something she didn't want to do.

'Adam, I'm sorry.' Her voice cracked, and she gave in to full-on sobbing.

He walked away from her and looked out of the window. Everything was normal out there, but his entire world had changed in less than five minutes.

How could one woman throw so many curveballs? She'd rejected his proposal, hinted at a secret she refused to tell him anything about, sprung a secret twin on him, told him she was pregnant and then told him she was getting rid of it without a second thought for his feelings. All this in the space of just shy of three months. He should have listened to his mates. He really was better off out of this.

28.

Adam drove on autopilot. He barely even registered where he was or where he was going. It didn't matter anyway. He couldn't stay in the flat a minute longer. She'd thrown the news about her being pregnant at him with such force and then clammed up straight away. After reading her diaries, it was obvious she could be open when she chose to be, which meant that she was deliberately holding back. Again.

He focused on the rhythmic sounds in the car – the windscreen wipers swishing back and forth and the ticking of the indicator – anything to keep him from thinking about the mess he'd left behind. He drove past a sign showing a turning for Cockfosters and switched his turn signal on, indicating to take it. Matt didn't live far away. He didn't want to tell him about the baby – there was no point since Sarah was so hell-bent on getting rid of it – but he needed some company, and Jenny and Carl were too caustic for him to deal with today.

Ten minutes later, he stepped through Matt's front door. He'd called on the way, and luckily Matt was home. Adam had always thought the reason why Matt rarely had people at his house was because he preferred to go out himself to escape for a while. Matt would always say it was too chaotic, but whenever Adam would walk through the house bearing gifts for his goddaughter, he'd wonder what all the fuss was about. Everything was always neat and tidy, and Molly was always clean and nicely dressed. Stopping by unannounced shattered that illusion.

Adam looked at the debris around him. How could anyone live like this? The floor was littered with multicoloured, plastic building blocks, and a seemingly endless number of dolls were scattered on the sofa. Sticky handprints covered the coffee table, and as he plucked a handful of dolls from the sofa to sit down, a tiny hand was thrust into his face, offering up squashed banana.

'Um, thanks.' Adam grimaced as Molly's plump hand deposited the slimy pieces of banana into his.

'Oh, that's rank,' Matt laughed, coming from the kitchen with a beaker full of juice and two cans of Coke. He handed Adam a pack of baby wipes. 'She does that all the time. Chews her food, spits it out and then hands it to you like it's a present. It's her new thing.'

Adam pulled out a wipe, scooped up the banana and grinned. 'Full of class, that one. Clearly she takes after you. How's things?'

'Same old. Trying to have a relaxing Sunday, but it's not really working.'

'I can come back another time? I don't want to interrupt.'

'What? Don't be silly. It's a pipe dream. There's no such thing as a relaxing Sunday for me anymore.' Matt raised his voice slightly above the noise of Molly singing and banging her toys together. 'What about you? Carl texted about your dad. How is he?'

'He's fine. He just has to manage his diet better, that kind of thing. The main thing is that he's okay.'

'I'm glad to hear it. He was always like a dad to all of us, your old man.'

'Yeah, I know.'

'How are things with Sarah?'

Adam took a deep breath. It was such a loaded question that it almost made his head physically hurt, especially since he didn't really know how to answer it.

'That bad, huh?' Matt said with a raised eyebrow. Clearly, Adam's silence spoke volumes.

'That bad,' Adam confirmed with a nod.

Matt picked up Molly as she tried to climb on his knee. 'Is she still giving you the cold shoulder?'

'The cold shoulder I could almost deal with. Now it's like Jack Frost has taken up permanent residence in the flat.'

'You're a better man than me. There's no way I could put up with that.' Matt moved his head to dodge the fingers trying to work their way up his nose. 'Molly, will you stop it?'

Adam couldn't help but smile as Molly laughed when Matt held her arms down. 'I suppose, but it's not going to be forever.'

Molly started to whimper, clearly frustrated at not being able to wriggle around freely, and seconds later the piercing sound of her crying filled the room. Matt put her down on the floor, and Adam winced at the screams bouncing off the walls. He looked at Molly, throwing her toys around, wailing at the top of her voice, before looking back at Matt. Christ, how did he cope?

'Is she all right?'

Matt waved his hand. 'She's fine. Just having a tantrum.'

He silently begged Molly to stop. It was so jarring that he couldn't concentrate on anything. It was like white noise. No way could he deal with that on a daily basis.

'What's wrong now?' Alice's voice floated down the stairs, swiftly followed by her appearing in the doorway, holding a towel in her hands.

'She's fine,' Matt said. Adam looked at Molly's red, tear-stained cheeks. She looked anything but, but who was he to judge?

Alice smirked. 'Yes, it looks like it. How are you, Adam?'

'I'm good, Alice. You?' Adam replied, standing up to kiss her cheek.

'Super, apart from having to sacrifice a nice soak in the bath to rescue my lovely fiancé from our terror of a daughter,' Alice said, playfully shoving Matt.

Matt rolled his eyes. 'I had it under control.'

'Looks like it.' Alice crouched down to pick up Molly, enveloping her in a hug, and blew raspberries into her neck. 'Come on, you cheeky monkey. Let's get you cleaned up. I'll leave you boys to it. Nice to see you again, Adam.'

'I'll pay for that later,' Matt said, shaking his head.

'Looks like hard work,' Adam said.

Matt bent down to clear some of the toys away and groaned. 'You have no idea. You should count yourself lucky you only have yourself to think about.'

'It is worth it, though, right?' Adam kept his voice neutral. He didn't want to sound like he was fishing for advice, which of course he was.

'Of course. I mean, don't get me wrong, there are times when I just want to walk out the door and never come back.' Matt threw the toys into a wicker basket and flicked the lid down. 'When she plays up like that, it's enough to drive me round the bend, but the tantrums, the noise and sleepless nights . . . They're worth it in the end. She's amazing.'

Adam looked at Matt's proud smile. It nearly leapt off his face.

'So when's the next one coming?'

'I didn't say I was crazy now, did I?' Matt laughed. 'I dunno. Alice wants another, but we'll see. Nothing's doing until Molly's a little older, in any case.'

'Yeah, she must keep you busy.'

'Just a bit. But I wouldn't change anything, and when I think back to how I felt when I found out Alice was pregnant, I honestly can't remember what all the fuss was about.'

Adam nodded. 'Yeah I remember. You were so worried about being tied down and losing your independence. Look at you now, Mr Family Man.'

'Tell me about it. Mortgage, kid, fiancée, hatchback – who'd have thought it?' Matt shrugged. 'There comes a time when we all have to grow up.'

'I guess.'

'I always thought you and Sarah would sort things out. I'm sorry it didn't work out.'

Adam shrugged. 'I asked her to marry me, and she broke up with me. I'd laugh if it wasn't so tragic.'

'Maybe you just shocked her. I mean, look at me. I was crapping myself at the idea of really settling down with Alice, even after three years. It's a huge step to get married. Maybe she just isn't ready yet.'

'Yeah, I thought that too at first, but I don't think it's that simple. It doesn't really matter now, anyway. It is what it is.'

Now that Adam knew Sarah was pregnant, his proposal was almost irrelevant, because even if he'd kept his mouth shut, they would still be in the same situation. She would still be pregnant, and she would probably still want an abortion. The look on Matt's face when he spoke about Molly and his proud megawatt smile had only helped convince Adam that he wanted this baby, or the option of having it, at least. He'd proposed, but in reality, he'd have been happy to be with her, without needing to get married. Now, he had nothing.

∽

It was past midnight by the time he got back home, and he assumed Sarah was asleep, but as soon as he sat on the bed, he heard a knock on the door.

'Adam?'

He looked up at the sound of Sarah's muffled voice through the door. What was she going to shock him with now?

He sat up on the bed. 'Come in.'

Sarah opened the door, tentatively stepped inside and closed it behind her. He crossed his legs to make space for her to sit, but she stayed where she was, standing with her back pressed against the door.

'I just wanted to apologise.' Her voice was small, and she kept her eyes on the floor. 'I was out of order earlier, when I said that the baby wasn't anything to do with you. I didn't mean it to sound how it did. What I meant was that I didn't make the decision not to keep it because of you.'

'I know. And I'm sorry for storming out like that. I just needed some space.'

Her shoulders dropped a fraction. If only he could say that he wanted her to keep the baby. He wasn't stupid; children were for life. He'd never be able to hand it back, and it would change both of their lives forever. Their relationship, if he could call it that, was in no fit state to bear the responsibility of a child. The idea of living on a daily basis with the noise and mess he'd caught a glimpse of at Matt's still made his stomach flip, but even so, the idea of her having an abortion?

Maybe it would have been better if she hadn't told him. It would have been an unspeakable thing for her to do, and in reality, chances were he'd never have been able to forgive her if she'd had an abortion without telling him first, but at least he wouldn't be sitting there, looking at her belly and thinking about the baby he'd never get to meet.

'Thanks.' Sarah paused as if there was more she wanted to say, and the tension of unspoken words was so present, he could almost feel the air crackling. 'I don't want to fight with you anymore. I really do wish things could be different.'

'It is what it is. It's not like anything's going to change, is it? I mean, you're still going through with the abortion, right?'

'You make it sound like I have a choice.'

'It's not like anyone's forcing you into it.'

Making peace felt like a woolly notion at best. Too much had happened. Their situation was so abnormal that the usual lines of a break-up had been blurred. They still shared the same flat, the same kitchen, the same toilet paper – everything. Up until a few days ago, they'd practically ignored each other. He'd had enough of feeling awkward in his own home. Sarah's aura of depression and secrecy had seeped through the flat, clinging to everything. It intertwined with every scrap of fabric and nestled in every corner of every room. It penetrated everything it touched.

When was the last time he'd heard her laugh? Santorini, probably, but he couldn't remember it. The disastrous last night had completely overshadowed the nine happy days they'd spent there. No matter how hard he tried, all he saw when he thought about Santorini was how she'd turned him down.

'I've decided to go up to Sheffield. There's a memorial service for Richard on Saturday, and I'd like to go.'

He nodded. So, she was going back home. Maybe she'd see her family.

'I can take you, if you want.'

'Oh, you don't have to do that. It's fine – I'll take the train,' she said.

'No, I want to.'

She frowned at him. 'Why?'

Adam shrugged. He wasn't entirely sure. He had no idea why he'd volunteered, but he had a feeling it had something to do with what Claire had said, about things pushing her to the breaking point. Everything was going to have to come to a head sooner or later. Maybe being back in Sheffield would help her get rid of whatever it was she was holding onto, and if it did, he wanted to be there when it happened.

'Do you really want to go on your own?'

She shook her head, and he shrugged again.

'So I'll take you.'

She gave him another small smile. 'Thanks.'

'And listen.' Adam cleared his throat. 'I'll support you whatever decision you make. You know that, right?'

She nodded. 'I know. And I'm really glad your dad's okay.'

She left the room and Adam sighed, lying back down on the bed. The words had felt like acid on his tongue. He always went with his instincts, and they were screaming at him to convince her to keep the baby, but it wasn't his decision to make. Despite everything, he still loved her, and that meant wanting her to be happy. It was obvious that this baby would bring her the complete opposite, and it would hardly be fair to bring a baby into their messed-up situation. It would be easier on both of them if he just went along with what she wanted.

29.

We're leaving for Sheffield in the morning. I was surprised that Adam offered to take me, but I guess my finally opening up to him has thawed things out a little, even if I haven't been able to tell him why I can't keep the baby. He looks at me differently, and it's harder for me to gauge what he's thinking. I don't want him to feel duty-bound to take me just because I'm pregnant, but I can't deny I'm relieved he'll be there with me. I don't want him to see all the crap I left behind, but I know I have to go.

Every time I think about it, my heart aches. I don't know what to expect at the memorial. The only funeral I've been to before was Dad's, and it was horrific. Seeing his coffin being lowered into the ground was like being engulfed by a deep black hole. I know it's a memorial service, so it won't be quite the same, but even so, I loved Richard. I loved Dad, of course, but it was obviously a different type of love. With Richard, my feelings were intense and raw, from the moment I met him until months after he left. It was fierce and all consuming. I remember how my skin used to burn when he touched me, how my heart would skip a beat when he looked at me. It was pure, heady teenage love.

I still can't believe he's dead. It's so strangely abstract. He was the boy I gave my virginity to. The boy who broke my heart by moving thousands of miles away and who impacted my life far more than he could ever possibly have known. The idea of him lying six feet underground is one I can't get my head around, but the fact is, I have unfinished business with him. If there's one thing I've come to realise in the last few days, it's that life is too short, whether it lasts forty-one years like my dad's or eight weeks like the baby I've just lost. It has to count for something.

I spent all of last night rereading my diaries from start to finish. For the last fifteen years, I've lived with this feeling of guilt and regret, but not once did I ever do anything about it. As I read them, all I could think was, what had taken me so long? What had stopped me from trying to locate him? I could have found him in minutes on Facebook. I could have contacted him if I really, really wanted to. Just like I could have been honest with Adam instead of hurting him. Now Richard will never know, and the guilt will never go away.

I have no one to blame but myself. If I'd told him, or my mum, or anyone what happened then, I might not be feeling this way now. I might have been more upfront with Adam to begin with. I might have been able to keep this baby and be happy instead of destroying everything around me like a nuclear bomb. Instead, I've written things down in bloody diaries that can't speak back.

I've been a coward. There's no other word for it. And it has to stop. I have to tell Adam. Even if he's moved on already, even if he doesn't love me, he deserves to be happy. I meant what I said to him last night. I don't want to fight with him anymore. Even after everything, he's still helping me out. I need to be honest with him. I owe him that much.

30.

Sarah was already up, showered and dressed by the time Adam stumbled into the kitchen for a coffee. They had plenty of time before they needed to leave but the way she sat on the arm of the sofa, with her handbag on her lap, told him she didn't want to hang around. She seemed impatient to get the day over with. Not that he could blame her. She must not have slept much because within minutes of hitting the motorway, she fell asleep, leaving him with just the radio for company.

He indicated left and began to slow down as he joined a slip road to a service station just outside Leicester. Two accidents and road works had caused long tailbacks, and it had taken almost two hours to get this far. According to his GPS, they only had around sixty miles to go, but he'd skipped breakfast and was in desperate need of some food.

He parked up, turned off the engine and looked at Sarah. She looked smart, in a plain, figure-hugging black dress and heels – a refreshing change from the jeans and Converse trainers she usually wore. He looked down at her stomach. When was the termination? She hadn't told him the exact date, but he guessed it would be soon.

The dull sound of raindrops hitting the car broke his train of thought. The sky had turned dark grey, and the rain clouds were merging upon one another, allowing minimal sunshine through. Within seconds, the light drizzle became a downpour. He watched the people who had previously been milling around the entrance, smoking, huddle under the shelter or jog back to their cars. No doubt the traffic on the motorway would slow down. They were pressed for time as it was.

He put his hand on her shoulder. 'Sarah.'

She jumped and opened her eyes. 'Are we here?'

She had an imprint of her bracelet on her cheek, from where she'd been resting on her arm.

'We're at the services. I need something to eat. Do you want anything?'

'Just some water, please.'

'You stay here,' he said as she went to take off her seatbelt. 'It's chucking it down. I'll be back in a minute.'

He got out of the car and jogged towards the entrance. It only took a few seconds, but the force of the downpour soaked him. His hair was plastered to his head, and his shirt clung to his skin. He grimaced. Why had the weather decided to turn just as he needed to get out of the car? The idea of continuing the drive in wet clothes wasn't particularly appealing.

After making his way up the stairs, he grabbed a sandwich and two bottles of water before joining the queue. The upper level of the service station spanned the motorway, and he looked at the flow of traffic beneath him. The spray of rainwater from the cars on the road was visible even from where he was standing, and the rain seemed to be getting heavier by the second.

He didn't bother to jog back to the car. There was little point since he was already soaked and the couple of seconds he'd save would hardly make a difference to their journey. As he approached the car, the passenger side door swung open, and a stream of vomit hit the ground.

He held the car door open and looked over the top as Sarah leaned out of the car. 'Are you okay?'

She shook her head and threw up again.

'Hold on.' He made his way round to the driver's side and sat beside her. 'Here.'

He held out a bottle of water, and she took it with trembling hands. She looked awful.

'You should have something to eat.'

She took a small sip of water and shook her head. 'I'm alright.'

'Having something in your stomach will stop you from feeling ill.' He held out half of his chicken and bacon sandwich. She shook her head again, but he kept his hand where it was. 'Take it.'

She looked at him for a few seconds before closing the car door and taking the sandwich.

'Are you okay to go?' he asked, putting his seatbelt on. She nodded back at him, and he turned on the engine, giving her the plastic bag, just in case.

He knew full well what was making her ill, but he wasn't going to be the one to refer to it first. He just hoped that they'd make it the rest of the way without needing to pull over for her to throw up again.

❧

Adam looked at the clock on the dashboard as they turned off the motorway. They were on the outskirts of Sheffield, and nerves had kicked in. He was nervous for Sarah and nervous about what the day was going to bring. He was sure he wasn't imagining the heavy weight of expectation that had been in the air since he woke up.

'Looks like we're going to be early. How far is the cemetery?' he asked.

'Not far. About fifteen minutes.'

She reached down for her handbag, and as she rifled through it, he caught a glimpse of the pink cover. His cheeks burned. She still had no idea that he'd read what she'd written on those pages, and once again he felt a wave of guilt rush over him for reading it.

'What do you want to do?' he asked. They had well over an hour before the service was due to start, and he didn't fancy the idea of hanging around in a cemetery.

She pulled a hairband out of her bag and twisted her hair up into a bun. 'I dunno. I should see Mum, I guess.' She shrugged. 'She doesn't live far.'

Adam nodded and allowed Sarah to guide him as they drove through to the city centre. So this was where she was from – a place with white and purple buses and trams trundling across the roads. What was she thinking? She'd gone so out of her way to hide this part of her life from him, and now they were here together. He couldn't deny the small thrill inside about her finally letting him in, even under these circumstances. They passed old factory buildings and warehouses with windows blackened by dust, grime and overgrown foliage. They had clearly seen better days, but as they approached the city centre, quiet, potholed streets gave way to roads with freshly laid tarmac and the gleam of new, modern architecture. He looked over at Sarah as she gazed out of the window. How long had it been since she'd been back here? It was possible that the city had changed so much in her absence that everything around them was as foreign to her as it was to him.

'You need to take the second exit,' Sarah said as they neared a large roundabout.

She bit her thumbnail as they drove up a hill, past a sprawling block of flats. He didn't need to ask if she was nervous, as her leg bounced up and down.

'Next left.'

He wanted to reach over and put his hand on her knee to calm her down. Instead, he followed her instruction and drove up yet another hill. The road wound around a series of bends, and he saw a large playing field against a panoramic view of the city. The rain hadn't stopped, but even through the curtain of drizzle, he could see the expanse of buildings and houses stretching into the distance. He could just about make out the green dome of Meadowhall Shopping Centre. He remembered seeing a picture of it in a geography textbook in school.

They followed the road round onto a street lined with identical semi-detached houses on either side, and somehow Adam knew that this was the street where Sarah grew up. She pointed ahead to a house with a neatly trimmed hedge and sloped drive.

'You can pull up there.'

He parked outside the house and turned off the engine.

'We're not staying for long. I want to get to the cemetery in time,' she said. Her voice sounded stilted, almost robotic, as if she were repeating a mantra.

Adam nodded. 'Sure. Whatever you want.'

He thought back to her diaries. This house held some unhappy memories for her, but he was intrigued to finally see it for himself. It was like her diaries were coming to life.

He'd made the right choice by offering to bring her up here. Something was telling him that this was exactly where he was supposed to be.

31.

Adam looked up at the house as he followed her up the sloped driveway. Red roses were carved into the mottled glass in the white PVC doorframe, but instead of going through the front door, Sarah opened the gate to the side of the house. The side door opened, and a woman with a dark-blonde bob stepped through, stretching her arms out.

'Sarah?'

Sarah looked awkward and strangely shy as she was drawn into a hug by the woman he assumed was her mum.

'I can't believe it's you!'

Adam couldn't miss the shock, excitement and heartbreak in her voice as she squeezed Sarah.

'Hi, Mum,' Sarah said in a quiet voice.

Sarah's mum stepped back and looked at her with a huge smile on her face. The resemblance between them was striking. She had the same amber eyes and heart-shaped face as Sarah and Claire.

Sarah turned to Adam. 'Mum, this is Adam.'

'Nice to meet you, Mrs . . .'

'Caroline,' Sarah interrupted him. 'Her name is Caroline.'

'Nice to meet you, Caroline,' Adam said, reaching out to shake her hand.

Sarah had cut in quite sharply, saving him. He had been about to call her Mrs Collins, but she'd probably taken Peter's name when she remarried.

Caroline smiled at him and looked at Sarah, obviously waiting for further information.

'I'm – er, a friend of Sarah's,' he said with what he hoped looked like a smile.

He tried not to let his shoulders sag with disappointment. It was clear that Sarah hadn't spoken to her mum for at least a year. Or if she had, she hadn't told her that she was in a relationship. There hadn't been a single spark of recognition in Caroline's eyes when he'd introduced himself.

'Well, come in,' she grinned, and they followed her into the warmth of the kitchen.

It was small and exceptionally clean. Not one thing was out of place, and it reminded him of a display in a kitchen showroom. A row of ceramic frogs sat on the windowsill behind the sink, and as he looked around, he saw more on the corner shelves at the end of the cupboard units. They all looked in pristine condition.

'You should have told me you were coming. I only spoke to Claire a few days ago, and she didn't mention anything about you coming up,' Caroline said in a broad accent, standing to one side and ushering them through to the hallway.

'It was a last-minute decision.'

'I would have sorted out some tea if I'd known.'

'I'm not hungry,' Sarah replied tersely.

'Okay,' Caroline said. Adam didn't miss the flicker of disappointment across her face. 'Would you like a drink . . . I'm sorry, what was your name again?'

'It's Adam,' he smiled, 'and yes, please.'

She nodded at him and gestured for them to go into the living room. Sarah stood in the middle of the room.

'Sit down, make yourself at home.' She smiled and left them alone in a room with more pictures on the walls than wallpaper.

He watched as Sarah walked around the room, looking at them all. He followed her path, looking at the images of Sarah and Claire, from babies to adults. How had she become so distant from them? From what he could see, they were a close family, for a while at least. There were pictures of Sarah and Claire on swings, holding ice cream cones on beaches, on bicycles, in gardens, in cars. As Sarah made her way around the room, the pictures of her seemed to diminish until they were only of Claire – graduation, parties and with Caroline. It was like Sarah had ceased to exist altogether.

She moved towards the fireplace and looked up at the clock ticking on the wall, with its pendulum swinging back and forth as the seconds quietly ticked by. She picked up a photo from the mantelpiece and stared at it.

'Do you want a cup of tea, Sarah?' Caroline called from the kitchen.

'No, I'm fine.' Sarah put the photo back, turned and looked at Adam as if she'd forgotten he was there. Her face turned red, and he looked away from her before sitting on the sofa.

He caught a glimpse of the photo Sarah had been holding: Caroline standing next to a man he presumed to be Peter.

Sarah sat next to him and put her hands in her lap. His family home exuded warmth. There didn't even have to be anyone in the room; there was just an air of comfort to it. This house was different. It felt dead somehow. He looked at the peach wallpaper and fluffy green carpet. Everything was neat and tidy, so much so that he couldn't imagine anyone actually living here. The television was on mute, and aside from the sound of Caroline making the drinks and the ticking of the clock on the wall, it was oddly quiet.

Caroline walked into the living room carrying a small tray holding three cups of tea and set it down on the coffee table. She picked one up and settled into the armchair.

'So, how are you, duck? What brings you back?'

Adam smiled to himself at the term of endearment.

'A friend of mine died. You remember Richard?'

Caroline looked up to the ceiling in thought.

'It doesn't matter.' Sarah sighed.

'Was he that boy you used to knock about with? From school?'

'I said, it doesn't matter.'

Adam swallowed a gulp of tea and shifted on the sofa. Every movement he made sounded amplified in the silence of the living room. The undercurrent of tension hung stale in the air. Maybe he should leave them to it. They clearly had things to talk about. Caroline looked at Sarah with sad eyes, and Sarah looked out of the window. It was a strange reunion. Why had Sarah suggested they come here when, from what he could see, it was the last place she wanted to be?

Caroline craned her neck to look out of the window. 'Peter's back.'

Sarah sighed. 'Great.'

So, he was about to meet Peter – Sarah's bogeyman. Adam listened as the side door opened and closed.

'Look who's here.' Caroline looked past Adam with a smile that looked like it could leap off her face. He turned to see Peter standing in the doorway, taking off his gloves.

'Sarah.' Peter smiled. 'What a lovely surprise.'

Adam waited for Sarah to reply, but she didn't. From the corner of his eye, he saw her pick up the cup of tea she'd initially declined.

'This is Adam.' Caroline shot Adam a small smile, triumphant at remembering his name. 'He's a friend of Sarah's. Adam, this is my husband, Peter.'

Peter shook his hand, and Adam tried to forget everything he'd read about him. Sarah had written in her diaries from the point of view of a teenage girl who hated her new father figure after the death of her dad. It wasn't surprising she didn't like him, but it wouldn't be fair to show any bias, especially when he wasn't supposed to know anything about their history at all. Peter took off his coat and sat in the empty armchair opposite them.

'Well, this is nice, even though we weren't expecting you.' Adam didn't miss that, even when met with Sarah's stony silence, Peter's smile didn't falter. In fact, he looked genuinely pleased to see them. 'So, Adam, how do you know our Sarah?'

Man. How was he supposed to answer that one? Adam looked at Sarah, but her face was expressionless. What was with her? It was like she was determined not to show any reaction to Peter whatsoever. Didn't she realise how awkward she was making everything? Adam hesitated. There was something about Peter that made him want to tell the truth.

After reading Sarah's diaries, he'd pictured Peter as a huge, imposing type of man, but now he'd met him for himself, Adam couldn't compute the image he'd had to the reality.

There was nothing intimidating about Peter at all. He was distinctly average – average height, average weight, average mousy brown hair, and he wore wire-rimmed glasses. He looked like the type of guy who wore shorts with socks and sandals in summer. In short, he looked harmless. Was this really Sarah's teenage nemesis? Peter looked at Adam before looking at Sarah and gave a small nod. His question had already been answered. Adam's silence had clearly told him that his relationship with Sarah wasn't straightforward.

'It's a shame Claire's not here as well,' Caroline said. 'It would be so nice to have my girls here together. It's been such a long time.'

'About nine years, isn't it?' Peter replied, looking directly at Sarah.

'She's working,' Sarah replied. It was the first time she'd spoken since Peter had come in the room.

'Sarah's here for a funeral,' Caroline said, looking at Peter. 'It's for that lad she used to knock about with after school.'

'Richard,' Sarah said. 'And it's not his funeral. It's a memorial.'

Peter nodded his head. 'Yes, I remember. We never met him, though, did we? Such a shame to die at such a young age. I'm sorry to hear the news.'

'I didn't think you'd care,' Sarah said, muttering into her cup.

'Of course I care. He was special to you, wasn't he?'

'You made my life hell when we were together,' Sarah replied, sounding every inch like the teenage girl Adam had read about in her diaries.

'That's not fair, Sarah,' Peter said, resting his elbows on the arms of the chair and interlocking his fingers.

Sarah waved her hand. 'Whatever. I know how I felt, and it was your fault.'

Caroline sighed. 'Sarah, please. It's such a treat for you to be here; let's not argue.'

'Well, stop acting like we're one big happy family then. Stop acting like you care.'

'Sarah.' Peter shook his head. 'Whatever you might think, you're a part of this family. You always have been, and you always will be.'

Sarah scowled and drank her tea. Adam had never seen her like this before, and he wanted to grab her by the shoulders and give her a shake. As far as he could see, Peter was being genuine, but Sarah was refusing to accept it. If there was one thing he knew about her, it was that she was as stubborn as hell, and he was beginning to think that she was doing nothing more than holding onto a grudge that she didn't need to keep.

Peter looked at Caroline. 'Darling, have you shown her the box yet?'

'No, not yet. I forgot. Come on, love. I've got something to show you,' Caroline replied, looking at Sarah.

Sarah sighed. 'What box?'

'We found some of the pictures you used to have up on your wall when we cleared out the loft. You know, the ones of you and all your friends? There's some of your dad in there too. We thought you might like to have them.'

Caroline smiled and held out her hand to Sarah. The box sounded like something nice to Adam, but from the way Sarah had been acting, he almost expected her to stomp out of the room as she followed her mum.

He heard them head upstairs and tried not to look at Peter. He looked out of the window, at the floor, at the walls and at the ceiling – everywhere but in Peter's direction. He didn't know what to say to him. The truth was, he felt sorry for him.

'So, what do you do then, Adam?'

Adam cleared his throat. 'I'm a property manager.'

'That's good. Something tangible, not like a lot of the young ones around here who don't seem to do anything at all. And what about Sarah? How's her job going?'

'Fine, I think. She doesn't really talk about it a lot. I guess it's one of those jobs where you want to switch off at the end of the day.'

Peter nodded. 'You've known each other for some time? I gathered there's some sort of history between the two of you.'

Adam ran a hand across his chin. 'It's complicated'.

'It always is.' Peter smiled. 'I know she sees me as the devil. The evil stepfather. She's always been difficult.'

Adam bit the inside of his cheek. He wasn't about to take sides in this argument.

'By all accounts, Sarah took her dad's death hard. Both of them did, but it was especially hard for her. She wasn't bubbly and open like Claire was. When Caroline and I first started courting, she was already self-destructive, and it got worse after we married and moved here. I thought I could help at first. Needless to say, every effort I made got sharply thrown back at me, and it's Caroline who suffered because of it.'

'How do you mean?' Adam asked.

'Has Sarah told you much about her family? That Caroline was an alcoholic?'

'No.' He shook his head. It wasn't a direct lie. He knew about her mum's alcoholism from her diaries, but Sarah hadn't actually told him anything.

Peter sighed, stood up and jammed his hands into his pockets as he walked to the window. 'Sarah was vulnerable back then. She'd lost her dad and moved to a new area. I suppose she started hanging around with a new group of friends, and soon she started staying out late and skipping school. It's normal teenage stuff, I know, but it became unbearable for Caroline. The constant arguments and resistance to discipline . . . It took its toll on her. Of course it's not only because of Sarah that she ended up drinking, but it certainly didn't help.'

'And now?' Adam asked.

'She's still an alcoholic. She always will be. It took a long time, but she doesn't drink anymore. I love the girls as if they're my own, but Caroline was always my number-one priority.'

'You helped her, then?'

Peter shrugged. 'It wasn't just me. It took a whole network of people, and she still goes to AA meetings. This *thing* with Sarah is hard on her. She misses a daughter who, for some unknown reason, has turned her back on her family. Nine years is a long time.'

Adam nodded, but what was he supposed to say? Sarah's diaries had implied that everything wrong with their family unit was Peter's fault. In them, Peter was the one who came between Sarah and her mum, grounded her, made her life unbearable and tried to control her, but what he was hearing now was very different.

'I just wish she'd let go.'

'Of what?'

'Everything. I tried to show her another way of dealing with her feelings. That there were people who could help, places she could go to. All this "making her life hell" that she goes on about.' He shook his head. 'She was a child becoming an adult, and she needed boundaries, like any other. It was as simple as that. I'd have thought she'd have realised that now, what with her job and all.'

Adam scratched the back of his neck. It was all at odds with what Sarah had written, and now he didn't know who or what to believe.

'I understand this is none of your business, really, but you're her friend, and I'd guess you're a close one. You seem like a decent lad, and I can tell you care about her. Maybe you can talk some sense into her. All of this animosity, it's killing her mother, and as nice as it is that she's come back today, it's going to affect Caroline, and Sarah's not going to be the one who has to deal with it all once she's gone. It's time for her to let it go.'

Adam nodded. 'I understand.'

Peter smiled, sat back in his armchair and turned the volume of the television up.

Why did Sarah hate him so much? Was it just on principle because her dad had died and Peter had moved in? Everyone had to deal with teenage angst at some point, but surely it was erring on the side of ridiculous to have kept it up for so long. He could see how Sarah's view of Peter could be skewed through no fault of his own. He wasn't stupid. There were always two sides to every story, and he didn't believe that Peter was totally innocent in what went on between them, but he was beginning to question whether Sarah had taken any responsibility for her part in what had happened.

He looked again at the pictures hanging on the wall. He couldn't help but feel for Caroline. How would she cope after they left, wondering whether she'd have to wait another nine years to see her daughter again? Would she start drinking again? No wonder the house felt joyless. He looked up at the ceiling. Sarah might see this as an obligatory visit, but Caroline had been waiting a long time for this. Whatever they were looking at up there, he hoped it would help.

A few minutes later, he heard footsteps coming down the stairs, and Sarah walked back into the living room.

'We should get going,' Sarah said, putting on her coat.

'Are you sure you can't stay?' Caroline asked, wringing her hands together. It reminded him of when Sarah had stood in his room and apologised for the things she'd said about the baby.

'We can't. We have to get to the cemetery,' Sarah replied and gestured to Adam.

Peter and Caroline walked them to the side door, and after saying goodbye, Caroline pulled Sarah into a hug. Adam raised his eyebrows. Sarah was hugging her back. Okay, so it wasn't a full-on bear hug, but it was an improvement on the one they'd had before, when Sarah had kept her arms firmly by her sides.

'Bye, Peter.'

The look of surprise on Peter's face must have mirrored Adam's. Less than an hour ago, she'd barely even acknowledged him. Adam held open the gate and watched Sarah as she walked through it. Something had definitely changed.

32.

Adam put his seatbelt on and looked at Sarah. 'You okay?'
'Yeah,' she replied, looking at him with a lopsided smile.
'What's that?' He looked down and saw her playing
with a piece of string.

'It was Richard's. He used to wear it as a bracelet. I thought I'd
lost it years ago.' She closed her hand around it and put it in her
pocket. 'It was in the attic with my stuff. Peter found it.'

He saw the confusion in her face.

'I didn't even think he noticed that I wore it.' She looked out of
the window. Caroline was standing by the gate.

'He seems nice. They both did,' Adam replied, looking out at
Caroline.

'Nice?' She looked down at the bracelet again and shrugged.
'Maybe.'

'Are you sure you want to go?'

'I have to. And we have to get back anyway.'

She put her seatbelt on, and he started the engine. As they drove
away, she craned her neck to look at Caroline waving them off until
they turned the corner.

◯

Sarah insisted that they park outside the cemetery. She wasn't sure exactly where the service would take place and wanted to wait in case she saw people she recognised. They didn't have to wait for long. Within minutes, a group of cars turned into the cemetery, and when a group of guys on skateboards whizzed past, she stiffened as if someone had stuck a rod against her back. She took Richard's bracelet from her pocket and held it in her hand as Adam started following the now substantial group of cars and skateboarders.

It was still raining, and with the radio turned off, all he could hear were car tyres crunching over gravel and the hypnotic sweep of the windscreen wipers. It reminded him of the clock in Caroline's living room with the pendulum swinging to and fro, like the windscreen wipers were counting down the seconds. Sarah stared straight ahead, playing with Richard's bracelet, wrapping it around her index finger, unravelling it and starting over again. Adam narrowed his eyes. A little part of him was jealous. It was ridiculous being jealous of a dead person, but he was. The way Sarah had reacted to the news of Richard's death made it obvious she'd never really got over him, and to make it worse, it wasn't like they'd split up because they'd fallen out of love. They'd split up because they'd been forced to, and it probably made everything seem that much more rose tinted. For all he knew, she could be sitting next to him, wondering what her life would have been like if Richard hadn't moved away. She could be wishing the two of them were married by now, with children, living happily ever after.

'Adam,' Sarah said firmly.

'What?'

'I said to stop back there.'

He looked down. He was gripping the steering wheel so hard that his knuckles had turned white.

He shook his head. 'Sorry, I was miles away.'

She looked at him with questioning eyes, and heat prickled the skin under his shirt collar. What was wrong with him? What kind of person felt jealous about a dead person? Ahead of them, the procession had stopped, and people were getting out of their cars.

It was a mixed crowd with people of all ages, Goths dressed head to toe in black and a group of girls wearing exceptionally bright dresses. The last of the skateboarders arrived, smoothly kicking the backs of their boards before grabbing them and coming to a stop in one fluid motion. It reminded him of a group of skaters he'd seen going up and down along graffiti-coated ramps on the South Bank.

'Just pull up here,' Sarah said.

'Why? It's raining and you don't have an umbrella. It would be better to go up there with everyone else.'

'No, I think I'll wait,' she said, twirling the bracelet around her finger.

Adam looked at the multicoloured crowd gathering on the wet grass. 'Am I missing something? I thought this is why we came here?'

'I'll go when I'm ready, Adam. Okay?'

He raised his eyebrows and stared at her. Would he ever understand her? She'd made such a fuss about coming, but now they were here, she seemed to have changed her mind.

He looked at the crowd through the cascading raindrops distorting the image through the window.

'You still love him, don't you?'

'Who?'

'Richard.'

She frowned and shook her head. 'Why would you say that?'

He continued to look out of the window and shrugged. 'He left because he had to, not because he wanted to. I know you still wanted to be with him, and I think you always have ever since.'

'What are you talking about?'

The pulse in Adam's neck throbbed. He couldn't keep it in for a second longer. 'I read your diaries.'

He turned to face her and steadied himself for the inevitable barrage of abuse that would be coming his way, but instead, Sarah stared back at him, blinking, with her mouth hanging open.

'You did what?'

'What did you expect, Sarah? You dumped me with no explanation, telling me there were things from your past that I didn't know about, and you refused to talk to me about it.' He sighed and rubbed his forehead. 'I didn't go hunting for them. I found them and I read some. It doesn't excuse what I did, but look at it from my point of view.'

She shook her head. 'Your point of view? You're telling me that you read my *private* diaries, and I'm supposed to look at things from *your* point of view?'

'If you'd been honest with me to begin with, I wouldn't have had to. I mean, for God's sake, look at how you've been acting. You've ignored me, told me you're pregnant and completely disregarded my feelings when you decided to have an abortion. If you'd been open with me in the first place, things might have been different.'

Adam winced as her hand whipped across his cheek. It took a second for him to register the fact that she'd slapped him. Hard.

'You bastard,' Sarah said, her chest rising and falling violently. 'On today of all days, you choose to come out with this? How dare you sit there acting all self-righteous? You went off and fucked someone else after, what – a month? You don't get to take the moral high ground.'

Adam sighed. There it was – the Tamsin-shaped bomb he'd hoped would never drop. He opened his mouth to speak, but Sarah put her hand up.

'Don't talk to me.' Her voice cracked as she grabbed her bag. 'Just fuck off, Adam.'

She got out of the car, slamming the door behind her. He watched her marching away from the car, and with every step she took, his breaths got shorter and shorter.

'Fuck!' He banged his fists on the steering wheel before running a hand through his hair.

Why had he told her about reading her diaries? What the hell had he been thinking? He swore again and looked out of the passenger window. Sarah was walking off into the distance, away from the crowd at Richard's grave and away from him.

His temples started to throb as blood and adrenalin rushed to his head. He looked around. What was he doing here anyway? He was miles away from home, sitting in a cemetery for the memorial service of someone he didn't even know, and his pregnant ex-girlfriend had just walked away from him for the second time.

He shook his head. 'Seriously, what the hell am I doing here?'

He turned the key in the ignition and turned the car around.

∾

Adam left the cemetery and followed the road down the hill. Why had Jenny told her about Tamsin? He clenched his jaw. As much as he wanted to be angry with Jenny, he wasn't. He was angry with himself, which was worse. Of course he'd been keen to sleep with Tamsin to begin with, but Sarah didn't know how he'd felt afterwards. She had no idea that he'd realised it was her he wanted, and nobody else. All she would have seen was that he'd slept with someone else less than a month after proposing.

The rain hit the car like bullets, rendering the wipers useless. As soon as they cleared one sheet of rain away, the windscreen was coated with another. To say it was turning out to be a miserable day was an understatement and a half.

He pulled over and looked at the seat next to him. Man, she'd got angry. He'd never seen her temper before, and despite the way he'd defended himself, she had every right to be as angry as she was. He'd read her diaries and stupidly told her about it as she sat looking at her first boyfriend's grave for the first time. Talk about bad timing. He unscrewed the lid off the bottle of water sitting in the cup holder and gulped it down in one go. He wiped the back of his mouth with his hand. The truth was, he'd wanted a reaction. Simple as that. He'd got jealous, angry and frustrated with all the secrets. It had felt like he'd just been taking her shit for far too long. Except now that he'd got a reaction from her, he felt like a complete arsehole.

How did she make him feel like this? If any of his exes had acted like Sarah had been acting lately, he'd have walked away a long time ago, but she'd got under his skin in a way that no woman ever had before. She wasn't perfect – far from it – but neither was he.

Sarah was different. He'd known from the start that she had something other girls didn't. She didn't care about makeup or clothes or money, and despite how she'd been acting lately, she was a caring person who tried to do the best by other people. He'd always sensed that she had something bubbling under the surface, something that she fought to keep a lid on – a kind of vulnerability – but he'd put it down to her job. She dealt with a heap of challenging things every day, and he'd reasoned with himself that dealing with the stress of other people's problems every day was why she sometimes looked like she was carrying the weight of the world on her shoulders. He knew it couldn't be easy, but she was dedicated to it, and he'd admired her for that. He'd loved her for it and he still did. But now, he wasn't so sure it was that simple. And even if it was, he'd learned that love wasn't enough.

A relationship needed more than that. It needed trust and respect, and both were in tatters. She'd hidden her past from him, and he'd gone behind her back and read her diaries – and that was just for starters. How could any couple ever get past the things they'd thrown at each other?

Adam rubbed at his eyes with the heels of his palms. Christ, when was the last time he'd cried? Probably when he'd broken his arm when he was thirteen. Crying just wasn't something that he did. But as he sat in his car on a hillside in a city he didn't know, the tightness of tears clogged his throat.

Everything was fucked. If it wasn't fucked before, it was certainly fucked now. He rubbed at his eyes again. He didn't want the tears to fall, but thinking about the girlfriend he'd lost and the child he was about to lose wasn't helping.

Broken trust, damaged respect. There was nothing holding them together anymore. His confession had snapped the last bit of thread between them. All he'd wanted was to get to the truth and hopefully get her back, but instead, he'd driven the last nail into the coffin containing their relationship.

He looked at the clock on the dashboard. They had a long drive back to London, and he was tired. He'd have to go back and get Sarah. He just wanted today to be over and done with, and as all they had to return to was a joyless flat, now was the time to admit defeat.

33.

By the time Adam turned back into the cemetery, the early winter evening was setting in, and the rain was so heavy that he had to switch his headlights on as he inched along the gravel driveway. Was this the spot he'd parked up in earlier? He was sure it was, but everyone had already left. He frowned, stepping out of the car, and walked over to where the crowd had gathered before.

The rain lashed his face as he read Richard's name inscribed into the square block of marble. Resting on top of the headstone was the string bracelet Sarah had been playing with. He looked around, but there was no sign of her. Maybe she'd already left.

He took his mobile out of his pocket and called her as he walked away from Richard's grave, but it rang out. She was obviously still angry with him, and he knew he'd disappointed her, which was even worse. No other woman would get anywhere near the kind of love he felt for Sarah. It had taken a bruised ego, a rebound fling and a slap around the face for him to realise that there was nothing to fight for anymore. Even the baby, the only real, tangible link between them, would soon be gone.

He sighed and wiped the rain from his face as he walked back to the car. He had a gym towel in the boot; he was sure of it. The sound of rain hitting the trees around him felt hollow and strangely far away as he wiped his face dry. He looked around. Was she still here? He had no idea how big the cemetery was, and he didn't want to play an endless game of cat and mouse, but he'd have to look for her. He didn't have a choice.

He drove along the pathway until it split in two. Which way had she gone – assuming she was even still here? He looked at the paths, alternating between left and right, and took the one on the left. Even with the heater on full blast, he shivered. He didn't see anyone as he crawled along the path. Maybe he really was the only one here. What a way to spend a Saturday – alone in a cemetery with just a car radio for company.

Was that her? He leaned forward and squinted. It was her, sitting on a bench with her back to him. Her cream coat stood out in the bleakness like a beacon. He killed the engine and sat watching her. She didn't turn around, but she must have heard him coming. He hoped she'd calmed down, at least enough for him to apologise and explain that he didn't need or want to know her secret anymore. He got out of the car and quietly closed the door. His eyes flicked over towards a bench up ahead. It didn't look like the others he'd seen dotted around the cemetery. Instead of legs, the smooth, dark-grey slab of stone sat on four cubes, two on either side. Each was painted a different colour and etched with letters from the alphabet.

Stepping away from the path and onto the grass, he began to make his way over to her. This bit of the cemetery felt very different. He stopped and crouched, resting the fingertips of one hand on the cold, wet grass as he looked at the elliptical black granite headstone by his feet, framed with a grey teddy bear. He looked at the dates beneath the name: 17 May 2009–17 May 2009. He shuddered and looked at the grave behind it. The wind curled itself around his neck as he looked at the image of Eeyore, the depressed yet loveable donkey from *Winnie the Pooh*. He swallowed and winced. He might as well have just swallowed a razor blade.

As he stood up to walk over to Sarah, all he could see were more and more headstones decorated with brightly coloured flowers and engravings of teddy bears and Disney characters. Goose bumps burst across his skin.

He tried not to think about the tiny bodies buried under the ground he was walking on. He'd always thought that death didn't freak him out. After all, it was inevitable and the only certain thing in life. There was nothing he or anybody else could do to stop it. Both sets of his grandparents had died before he was born, and it was only when his dad had suffered his TIA that death became something a lot less abstract and a lot more real. Being here was making his underarms prickle with anxiety.

He couldn't even begin to think what the parents of these kids had gone through. He shook his head and jammed his hands further into his pockets. Just thinking about it made his stomach turn. Was a miscarriage, or even an abortion, much different? Okay, so he'd never actually see his baby, but did that make it any less worse? Maybe Sarah was doing them a favour by having an abortion. At least that way, they would never have to experience the pain of losing their child. There'd be no memories to haunt them.

Sarah flinched as the crunch of leaves under his thin-soled leather shoes echoed around them, but she didn't turn around. She was sitting in front of a statue and was so still, she might as well have been made of stone herself. A gust of wind blew towards him, and he got a hint of her shampoo. It was funny how a smell could sum up a person. He knew that if he smelled it again years down the line, it would always bring up the image of Sarah in his mind.

He went and sat next to her. He wanted to turn and look at her, but he forced himself not to. Instead, he looked at the statue a few feet in front of them.

It was small – three, maybe four feet high, and as he studied it in detail, he saw the signs of weathering. The small, pockmarked holes reminded him of the woodworm infestation they'd had in his family home when he was about seven years old. His dad had been renovating the house, and Adam had begged his father to let him help. When they'd pulled back the carpet to reveal the rotting floorboards underneath, his dad had sworn. Thinking about it, it was perhaps the only time he'd ever heard his dad curse, but while his dad was annoyed with the infestation, Adam was fascinated. The statue, carved from a single block of stone, made him feel the same way.

It was beautiful, but there was something heartbreaking about it. He looked at it, taking in every detail of the kneeling angel resting her head on her arm. Her eyes were closed, and the corners of her mouth turned up with the hint of a serene smile, like a stone Mona Lisa. A wing curled its way around her shoulder protectively, resting in her lap. He looked at its chubby limbs and cheeks. Was it an angel or a cherub? He didn't know the difference, but either way, it stood almost like a guardian of this section of the cemetery.

He rubbed his hands over his mouth and tipped his head back, blinking a few times until the moisture in his eyes receded. He turned and looked down at Sarah, studying her profile. He looked at the slight upturn of her nose, the shape of her lips and her eyelashes resting on her cheekbones as she kept her eyes closed. She was holding a small rectangular tin in her hands, decorated with swirly patterns.

Everything around them sounded sharp in the quietness of the cemetery – a bird chirping somewhere in the trees, the rustling of dead leaves on the ground being pushed along by the wind. Sarah's breathing. It was so quiet, he was convinced he'd have been able to hear her heartbeat if he listened long and hard enough.

Finally, Sarah opened her eyes and looked back at him. Her eyes were red-rimmed, puffy and seemed to be searching for something as the intense amber of her irises scanned his. He blinked. She still had the power to make his mind blank with just a look. Was she still angry with him? What was she doing here anyway? It was a peaceful place, but it was hardly somewhere most people would choose to relax.

'You came back,' Sarah said in a voice so small it might as well have been a whisper.

'Of course I did.'

He looked down at his feet. His shoes were speckled with rain and mud, and his toes were cold. He wriggled them in his shoes to try to inject some warmth.

She folded her arms and hunched her shoulders to her ears. 'I shouldn't have slapped you earlier. I'm sorry.'

He knitted his eyebrows together. 'I deserved it. What I did was unforgivable. You had every right to be angry.'

'It's lovely, isn't it?' she said, nodding towards the statue. 'It was put up in remembrance of an abandoned baby, you know.'

Adam looked at the statue and grimaced. Just when he thought this place couldn't get any grimmer.

'I like it here,' Sarah continued. 'I feel like I can think here. It's funny. I've spent so long trying to forget, but now that I'm back, all I want to do is remember.'

Adam frowned and took his hands out of his pockets. Trying to forget what? And did he really want to know? He'd only just resigned himself to never knowing what her secret was, and after yo-yoing backwards and forwards for months, he didn't have the energy for it anymore. He'd thought that finding out her secret would be the answer to all their problems, but now he knew better. Her secret was never going to be the glue to put their relationship back together, and as selfish as it might have been, he didn't want to know her secret anymore. There was only so much two people could take.

Sarah leaned forward, picked off a small snail making its way up the statue and put it down on the grass. 'If anyone should be angry, it's you. You've put up with so much from me.'

Adam shrugged.

'At first, I thought you coming up here with me was the worst thing that could have happened, but it got me thinking. It made me realise that I don't want to hide this part of my life anymore.'

As she turned to face him, Adam swallowed. After waiting and hoping for her to open up for so long, he wanted to clamp his hand over her mouth. Being here was freaking him out. She was freaking him out.

'It's fine,' he said and looked away. 'You don't have to tell me anything. Really. It's none of my business anyway.'

'It is, though.'

'Seriously, Sarah. There's really no point. I get it.

'At the very least you'll understand why I can't keep the baby.'

He frowned. Even if she did tell him the truth, she'd still do what she wanted as far as the pregnancy was concerned. He was beyond hoping for happy endings.

'If you really want to tell me everything, then I'm not going to stop you, but I don't want to sit here any longer than I have to.'

'We could go back to the car,' Sarah suggested. He looked down at her hands. She was holding the tin so tightly that her knuckles almost popped white in her skin. 'I really need to talk, Adam. It won't take long.'

He looked up at the sky and clenched his jaw. He was beyond tired. It felt like the longest day of his life, and now it was about to get longer, but if he turned away now, after she'd explicitly told him she wanted to talk, he'd feel like a total prick.

He looked at his watch. 'Okay. We passed a hotel by that roundabout. I'm really tired, and I'd rather not drive back tonight. We can get some dinner and dry ourselves out. Then we'll talk.'

Sarah nodded slowly. 'Okay.'

He was sure it couldn't have been easy to decide to finally tell him everything, but he'd have been lying if he said he wasn't relieved at having found a way to put it off a little longer.

34.

The heat of the hotel lobby wrapped itself around Adam like a blanket. After the cold and rain of the cemetery, he felt like he could collapse on a bed and sleep for days. He asked the receptionist for two rooms, trying to ignore the way his eyelids scraped over his eyes when he blinked. He was exhausted, and the warm air was making them dry.

The receptionist smiled up at him. 'Do you have a reservation?'

Was she for real? Why would he have asked for the rooms if they had a reservation? He began to drum his fingers on the polished teak desk before stopping himself. It wasn't – he peered at her name badge – it wasn't Leanne's fault that he was dog tired after spending the day driving on the motorway, sitting in a tension-packed living room and hanging around in a cemetery.

He shook his head. 'Is that a problem?'

'Not at all,' she replied, tapping her fingers on the keyboard in front of her.

He looked down at her nails. They were long and intricately painted with a swirly design and little diamante crystals stuck on the ends. He looked over at Sarah's hands, pressed against the edge of the desk. She used to bite them when they first met, especially when she was nervous. Her fingertips were red. The thought of covering them with his and warming them up flew across his mind.

Instead, he reached inside his jacket and took out his wallet. He took out his credit card and put it on the desk in front of them.

Two hundred pounds later, Adam closed the door to his room behind him and slotted the key card into the holder on the wall. His damp shirt was stuck to his back, his toes were numb and his left eye pulsated with a dull throb. He looked at the bed and pictured himself flopping onto it, falling into a deep sleep and fast-forwarding to tomorrow. The day had unfolded like a disjointed film that made no sense. It was making his head spin.

He'd suggested they take a shower and freshen up, but neither of them had anything to change into. It was all a delay tactic. He couldn't miss the irony of the situation. For ages, he'd thought of nothing else. The intrigue of Sarah's secret had driven him to read her diaries, kept him awake at night and distracted him at work. Now, here she was, ready to open up to him, and he was swatting her away like a fly.

He undressed, draped his suit over the back of the chair by the desk and walked into the bathroom. Leaning one hand against the wall by the mirror, he looked at his reflection and ran a hand across the dark stubble on his cheeks. After today, there would be no going back. He hadn't thought much beyond finding out what her secret was, but now all he could see was an empty space. Finito. The End. It was really happening. In less than a month, it would all be over. They would have left the flat, and there would be no more Adam and Sarah, no secret, no baby. Nothing.

He turned on the shower and stood under the hot spray of water, letting it cascade down his head and onto his shoulders. It was almost unbearably hot, but within seconds, his muscles began to relax, and the cold that seemed to have set right into his bones slowly thawed out.

Up here in Sheffield, they were removed from normality – if he could call the tension that had taken over their daily lives normal. Not having to carry that tension around anymore was what he'd wanted all along, but he wasn't stupid. Whatever it was she had to say to him wasn't going to be pretty; otherwise, she'd have told him what it was ages ago. It wouldn't have had to take the death of her friend and standing in a children's cemetery to do it. It would change the way he saw her; he was sure about that.

୬

Adam sat on the foot of Sarah's bed and looked around at the room. It was identical to his. She'd even draped her dress over the back of the chair, just like he had done with his suit. He looked at her, sitting up, leaning against the headboard. They were in matching fluffy white towelling robes, and he'd have forgiven anyone looking in from the outside for thinking that they were just an average couple, eating room-service sandwiches in their shared room. She dabbed the crumbs on her plate with her finger, and he tried not to focus on the small, delicate curls at the nape of her neck. God, she really was gorgeous.

She put her plate on the tray on the floor and looked at him. He was all out of excuses to put it off any longer. They'd eaten their sandwiches in silence, with the television turned on and the volume low in the background. He hadn't thought about anything as he ate. He'd wanted to empty his mind of everything and found it surprisingly easy.

She sighed. 'So, I've been thinking about how to say all this, and I still have no idea how to start.'

Adam raised one side of his mouth to give her what he hoped was a sympathetic smile, when all he wanted to do was say, 'Don't. Don't tell me, I don't need to know.' But he couldn't do that. It would damage her beyond imagination if he did. The last piece of the sandwich he'd swallowed seemed to be stuck right in the middle of his throat, and his attempts to swallow it down did nothing.

'You said you knew about Richard, from reading my diaries.'

His cheeks and ears burned. 'Sarah, I—'

'I need you to not talk. Otherwise I'll never get this out.'

He raised his eyebrows and nodded. Had she just told him to shut up?

'Believe it or not, I'm not actually angry that you read them. I mean, I was at first. Of course I was. I couldn't believe that you'd gone behind my back like that. But it wasn't really you that I was angry with. I was angry at myself.'

She drew her legs up to her chest, wrapping her arms around her knees.

'I know that none of this has been easy for you, and I am really sorry for the way I've been acting. You really didn't deserve any of it, but I was so scared of telling you the truth, and then when I found out about Richard, it all just got too much. The baby . . . you . . . him.' She shook her head. 'But I can't lie anymore. Even if you walk out of here and never want to lay eyes on me again, you need to know.'

Adam swallowed. Jesus Christ. What was she about to tell him? His heart started to ram against his chest as if it were trying to escape. It had the right idea. It was exactly what he wanted to do himself. Instead, he forced himself to stay put on the bed.

'This isn't the first time that I've been pregnant. I had a baby when I was fifteen. A boy. Jack.'

Adam screwed his eyebrows together and shook his head. She had a kid? He clamped his teeth together to stop his jaw from hanging open. He looked at her, huddled against the headboard with her eyes wide open and staring at him. She had a child. A son. A *fifteen-year-old* son. Never mind keeping Claire a secret – this was huge.

He cleared his throat. 'With Richard?'

Sarah nodded. He nodded back and looked out of the window as the pieces of the jigsaw slowly slid into place. Suddenly, her reaction to Richard's death didn't seem so extreme.

'Okay. So where is he now? Did you put him up for adoption?'

She chewed her bottom lip and reached down to the floor for her handbag. Her hands shook as she pulled out the tin she'd been holding in the cemetery.

She looked down at it and slowly ran her fingers over the lid. 'I found this when I was up in the attic earlier with Mum. I've never shown this to anyone before.'

It didn't look like she wanted to now either, not if the way she was clinging onto the box was anything to go by.

'Here.' She held her arm out and looked away. He swallowed as he took it from her.

It was only a tiny box, but whatever was in it clearly held a lot of weight. He looked down at the black tin. Her secret, the thing that had been the root cause of their break-up, was right there in his hands. He pushed his thumb under the lid and popped it open.

35.

Adam lifted one of the loose, torn sections of newspaper from the box and unfolded it. A frown spread across his face as his eyes scanned the paper in front of him.

Police appeal to mother of abandoned baby boy.

He looked at Sarah, but she kept her eyes fixed firmly on the floor. Why did she have this stuff? He picked out another paper clipping.

Dead baby discovered outside Hallamshire Hospital.

South Yorkshire police concerned for baby's mother . . . May be in need of urgent medical assistance.

Memorial service to be held for abandoned baby boy, named Alfie.

His blood ran cold. He'd always thought it was just a saying, but it really did feel like every bit of his body had just been blasted with ice.

'Sarah?' His eyes flicked from the newspaper clipping in his hand to Sarah and back again. 'What is all this?'

'His name was Jack,' Sarah whispered.

Adam screwed his eyebrows together and shook his head. 'It says his name was Alfie.'

'Alfie was the name of the nurse who found him.'

'Are you telling me that *this*' – he held up the paper in his hand and swallowed – 'is about *you*?'

The steady thump of his heartbeat echoed in his ears as he looked at her. Out of all the scenarios he could ever have dreamt up to try to guess what her secret was, it definitely wouldn't have been this. But when she looked up at him, he knew. It was written all over her face – in the tears streaming down her cheeks and her wobbling chin.

Jesus.

'I don't understand,' Adam said, rubbing his hands over his face. There were too many things going round in his head all at once, and he needed to make them stop. 'I mean, I don't get how this could be about you and how the hell I didn't know about any of it.'

'I didn't know how to tell you.' She wiped the tears from her face with the sleeve of her pristine towelling robe. 'But then I found out I was pregnant, and then I heard about Richard and . . .'

'Did he know?'

Sarah shook her head and bit the inside of her cheek. 'I never got the chance to tell him.'

'Did he even know you were pregnant?'

'No.' She pulled her knees up to her chest and wrapped her arms around her legs. 'He moved away. You know that from reading my diaries.'

'You still could have contacted him.'

'I know that now, but back then, I couldn't. Whenever I'd start to get upset about him leaving, I'd tell myself it was only a few hundred miles away and that we'd write to each other and speak on the phone. That he'd come back to see his grandparents – it wasn't like I'd never see him again. We'd spoken about it and promised to stay together until we could be together, you know? But when I'd lie in bed at night, I'd panic. It wasn't just a few hundred miles. It was three thousand, eight hundred and thirty-seven. I'd looked it up in the library. I had Claire, but I didn't know how I'd survive without him being there. Mum was losing herself in booze every night, and Peter went from being overbearing to acting like I didn't exist at all.'

'Okay,' Adam said slowly, shaking his head. 'But what does that have to do with—'

'You know, this would be a lot easier if you just let me talk.'

'Okay.' He nodded and she exhaled loudly.

'It took years for me to realise how angry I was back then. I hated Peter because he wasn't my dad, and I made Mum's life hell. I knew that with Richard gone, I'd have to spend every day dealing with the crap at home with nothing to look forward to and no one to make me feel better. He'd become the most important person in my life so quickly, and then, one day, he was just gone. I spoke to him on the phone the morning he left, and it was the last time I ever heard his voice. For all our intensity, it fizzled out almost straight away. For him, at least.

'I used to sit by the phone every night, hoping he'd call. I'd stay up for as long as I could. New York is five hours behind, and I didn't want to miss him when he called. But he never did. And just when I started to think he'd forgotten all about me, I got a postcard. It didn't say very much, but for the first time since he'd left, I had a smile on my face. The world could have ended that day, and I wouldn't have cared. I wrote back to him straight away. I was so fuelled on adrenalin that I can hardly even remember what I wrote now. That was the last contact we had.

'Looking back, I can't blame him. I mean, he'd just moved to one of the coolest cities on earth. He would have been making new friends and having fun, but I couldn't see it like that at the time. All I knew was that it felt like my world had ended. I'd sit on my bed listening to music with tears streaming down my face, trying to understand what I'd done wrong – what was wrong with me. Why I wasn't good enough to keep him interested even for a few weeks after being apart. I started to question whether I'd imagined how our relationship was.'

Adam nodded. He knew the feeling well. He might not have cried himself to sleep, but he'd asked himself the same questions since he proposed.

'I went wild after that,' Sarah continued. 'There's a whole chunk of time where I can barely remember anything. I'd go out, even when I had nowhere to go, and I started drinking. I put everyone through hell – Mum, Claire, even Peter. I'd go to school, bunk off for most of the day and come home drunk and stoned, way past my curfew. I was a nightmare, and I knew I was taking things too far, but I couldn't stop. I was so blinded by how I felt that nothing else mattered. Even Claire couldn't get through to me. We'd become so close, but I just wasn't interested in what she had to say.

'I'd been on an almost constant binge for about four months when I realised my periods had stopped. They weren't regular any-way, but I knew it wasn't normal, and I'd put on weight. At the time, I thought it was all the alcohol and junk food. I just didn't think it could be anything else. We'd used condoms, but I guess we were just unlucky.

'I was terrified. I was only fourteen and I was pregnant, and all I could think about was how disappointed Mum would be. Never mind the booze and the drugs; this was something on a whole new level. I thought that at least if Richard was there, we could have faced it together. So, I wrote to him. I wrote a stupidly long letter, telling him how much I loved and missed him. I didn't say anything about the baby. It's hardly something you tell someone in writing, is it? But I thought that if I poured out everything that was in my head, it would get him to remember what we had. That it would get him to remember *me*.

'I stopped drinking and smoking. I really cleaned myself up, and I knew how relieved Mum was because, from the outside looking in, it must have looked like I was almost back to my normal self. I'd decided not to tell anyone about the baby until I heard back from Richard. I guess I needed to know that he still loved me and I wouldn't be alone, because it would make disappointing Mum and having everyone think I was a slag so much easier.'

Adam grimaced. Richard never came back. She would have gone through the pregnancy by herself.

'Didn't anyone notice?' He frowned. 'I mean, a bump must get a little hard to hide.'

She shook her head. 'I wasn't exactly skinny to begin with, and I'd been living in baggy jeans and oversized hoodies for ages.

'I started to realise that I wasn't going to get a reply. I tried to tell myself that my letter must have got lost in the post, but I knew, even then, that it was a stupid excuse, because I didn't write to him again. It was like I was stuck in this weird place where it wasn't really happening. Nobody else knew about it, and I started to think that maybe it was a good thing because things like that just didn't happen to people like me. Stuff like that only happened to other people, and if it had to happen to me, then I wanted to be able to say that I wasn't alone, that Richard would stand by me one hundred per cent – and I couldn't, so the best thing for me to do was ignore it.

'Then Hannah let slip that Richard had been in touch with Daniel. Apparently, he was having a great time going to parties, making new friends and he had a new girlfriend. I felt like such an idiot. I went home that day and I came this close to telling Mum.' Sarah held up her hand and pinched her thumb and forefinger together. 'I knew that I'd screwed up in a big way, and I didn't know what to do about it, but I couldn't say anything. For the first time in a long time, she seemed like she was happy. I didn't want to be the one to wreck it, and going by how Peter had reacted when I started seeing Richard, I was too scared to say anything. I thought he might kick me out, and I'd be on my own with a baby to look after. So, I decided not to say anything about the baby until it was too late. My skewed logic told me that once I'd had the baby, it would all just work out somehow.'

Adam shook his head. 'You were just a kid, Sarah. There's no way they'd have thrown you out. They love you – even I can see that, and I've only met them once.'

'I know that now. But I couldn't think straight. All I knew was that I was fourteen and pregnant and alone. They were born again Christians. Sex before marriage just wasn't acceptable to them. They'd told me and Claire that plenty of times.'

'Why didn't you tell Claire? She would have stuck by you. I barely even know her, but I know that much.'

'Because she would have made me do something about it. Tell Mum, have an abortion – something. She's always been the 'doer' out of the two of us.'

'And you just wanted to stick your head in the sand?' Adam looked out of the window.

Claire had been right about Sarah. Imagine keeping something so big from everyone and hoping it would somehow magic itself away.

Sarah shrugged and picked at a loose thread on her towelling robe. 'Basically.'

Adam puffed the air out in his cheeks and looked at the tin box sitting in the vast space between them on the bed. Who knew something so small could contain something so big? But it still didn't explain how the baby she'd given birth to had ended up dead.

36.

'I could really do with a cigarette right now,' Adam said, tapping his fingers against his legs. He would never describe himself as a smoker, not really. He only smoked when he was drinking. Come to think of it, he could do with a drink too.

'I know it's a lot to take in,' Sarah replied, and Adam half-laughed to himself. Slight understatement. 'But if it's any consolation, it's just as hard for me admitting all this as it is for you to hear it.'

Adam shrugged. She had a point. 'So, what happened? You had the baby and then what? The paper article said he was . . . you know.'

'I was about seven and a half months pregnant when I went into labour. I'd woken up feeling awful, and at first I thought it was flu or some kind of bug. I went to school, but I felt sick to my stomach and my back ached. I made it through until the second-to-last period – French class. I sat there telling myself that I couldn't be in labour. I'd seen films with labour scenes, and this was nothing like that. I actually told myself that because I didn't feel the need to push, nothing was happening. In fact, it actually felt like period pains to begin with, but then, after class, I went to the toilet, and my waters broke, and it was like someone had slapped me across the face. It was real and it was happening, whether anyone knew about it or not.

'I grabbed Claire before she went into her next lesson. I didn't know what else to do. All I knew was that I had to get out of there, and I couldn't do it alone. When I told her what was going on, she got so angry, but when I doubled over, she took charge like I needed her to. I was in a complete panic. I hadn't looked into childbirth at all. I still had over a month before I was anywhere near due, and it wasn't like it is now – there was no Google or YouTube video to walk me through it. I don't know what I would have done without Claire.

'She took me to The Rec – an old cricket pavilion in a park. It was where the sixth formers and cool kids used to hang out in the summer. It was raining and cold, and I guess Claire thought it was the best place to go.

'I hadn't been timing my contractions. I hadn't thought to, but they were getting pretty regular. I felt like I'd tripled in weight, I was so heavy. Every contraction got worse than the last, and I didn't know how long it would go on for, or how long *I* could go on for, but Claire was fantastic. We were totally unprepared – we didn't have anything. I was lying on my school blazer and Claire had a bottle of water. That was it.'

'That's insane.' Adam shook his head. 'Christ, you could have died, Sarah. Why didn't you just go to the hospital?'

'She wanted to call an ambulance, but I begged her not to. The nearest phone box was at least twenty minutes away, and I was too scared to let her out of my sight. I wanted to be anywhere else but there, but if that was where I had to be, then I needed her with me.

'It was the most surreal experience I've ever had. It was the day before my fifteenth birthday, and I was about to give birth in a falling-down cricket pavilion in the middle of a park, with only my sister there to help. To this day, I still don't know how she held it all together, but she did. I could see in her eyes that she was just as scared as I was, but she kept me calm. We had nothing to go on except for films and TV shows we'd seen, and that meant pushing. And even when I knew I had to, when my body was begging me to, every instinct I had wanted to do the exact opposite. In the end I had to. It was the worst pain I've ever felt, and for a minute, I really did think I was going to die. And then . . .' Sarah wiped her eyes and smiled for the first time in what felt like forever. 'And then, he came.'

'Jesus.' Adam ran a hand over his mouth and swallowed. It was barbaric. It was the kind of thing he would expect to hear about in a third-world country, not Yorkshire.

'Something was wrong, we knew that straight away,' Sarah said, shaking her head with her eyes focusing on the wall behind him. 'The look on Claire's face . . . I'll never forget it. It was like she'd literally seen a ghost. She looked terrified, and for a minute I wondered if there was something wrong with me until I saw her holding my baby in her coat.

'His little face . . . It was so tiny. He was the most beautiful thing I'd ever seen, with skin so fine, like glass. But he wasn't crying. He wasn't moving at all, and his eyes were closed.

'I'd never seen a dead body before. Not even Dad's. Mum said we were too young to see him when he was at the funeral home. But I knew my baby was dead. All my energy rushed back at once, and I grabbed him from her. When his head lolled back, I got this feeling in the pit of my stomach. It was like a ball of every bad feeling you could imagine, all rolled into one, like the worst kind of sickness. I could hear this noise, like an animal trapped in barbed wire, and it wasn't until Claire put her arms around me that I realised it was me.

'I don't know how long we stayed there for. We just sat there, holding him, and all I could think was, *It's my fault*. All the drinking and smoking – it was my fucking fault. I'd killed him because I was too fucking drunk and drugged up to even realise I was pregnant in

213

the first place. I'd killed the last bit of Richard I had. I didn't know what to do. It would have been hard enough telling Mum and Peter about the baby anyway, but telling them that I'd killed him was something I couldn't do. No way. I'd burn in hell for all eternity. I didn't need Peter to tell me that – I knew it for myself.

'I called him Jack. I hadn't thought about names at all until then, but when I held him, I knew that was his name. His skin was so soft. I ran my fingers over his eyebrows, his little button nose and across his cheeks. I buried my face in his head with his downy baby hair tickling my nose, clinging to the hope that he was just asleep and he'd open his eyes. But he didn't. They say that a person's eyes are the windows to their soul. I never got to see his.

'We had no idea what to do. It was late, it was freezing cold and eventually we decided that the hospital would be the best place for him because they'd know what to do. All we had was Claire's gym bag, but I couldn't put Jack in there myself. I just couldn't. I had to sit there as Claire took him from me and put him in the bag. My mind was starting to scramble. I was worried he'd suffocate, and all I could think about was him wondering why he was being stuffed into a smelly old bag in the dark where he couldn't breathe.

'I didn't look when she zipped the bag up, and she had to physi-cally manhandle me to get me up off the floor. I must have looked a complete state, but nobody paid us any attention. We were walking down the street with my dead son in a bag, and nobody noticed.

'When we got to town, Claire left me to go to the hospital, and I carried on home. It sounds really heartless to say that out loud, but I couldn't have gone with her. I got home, and Mum and Peter were asleep. It's funny. If I'd come home that late a few months earlier, there would have been hell to pay, but as far as they were concerned, I'd sorted myself out, was back to my normal self. I didn't even have a curfew anymore. And you know what? I would have really loved one. I would have loved to have walked through the door and seen them waiting for me at the table, because then they would have known something was wrong. But I didn't. I had a bath and went to bed and cried like I've never cried before. I cried so much I made myself sick.

'When Claire finally came home, she got into bed with me, and we just held each other. She told me she'd left him outside the hospital and called the reception from a payphone. She promised me he'd be looked after, and the doctors and nurses would know what to do. I don't think I could ever tell her how much it meant to me that she did what she did. It was the early hours of our fifteenth birthday, and it had been spent covering up the death of my secret baby. Because of me, we'd never be able to celebrate a birthday again without thinking about what happened.

'The next day, it was reported on the morning news. They said he'd been dumped, as if I'd never wanted him. As if I didn't care. It was in the newspaper too. The way they reported it made me sound like a monster, because they weren't sure if he'd died before or after being left at the hospital. That really hurt. I loved him. There's no way I'd have dumped him to die; he was already dead. It didn't excuse what I'd done, but sitting there, watching it on TV, it felt like a witch-hunt. I already knew it was my fault that he'd died, and they did too. I was scared I'd end up in prison or something, and Claire too. So we made a pact. Neither of us would tell what had happened. We wouldn't say anything to Mum, Peter or the police. And we've never spoken about it since. Even now, we always talk to each other on the day it happened, but we never actually speak about it, and we never mention his name.

'We might never be the closest of sisters, but she was the one person I could rely on. She'd held it all together so well, but I was weak. I always had been. We got tattoos a few years later to remember him by. It was Claire's idea, actually. She acts so strong, but I know how much it broke her. I was the only one who knew why she'd zone out sometimes. I knew that when she'd go quiet, she was thinking about him.

'I've tried to make it better ever since. That's why I became a social worker. It sounds so cliché, but I didn't want what happened to me to happen to anyone else. At the time, I convinced myself Mum and Peter would throw me out and disown me, but seeing what I see every day at work, I know they're nothing like that. Going back today was . . .' She shook her head. 'I don't know. Maybe I underestimated them. Maybe we'd have coped if I'd told them the truth, even if the end result would have been the same.

'Work was a way to try and make it all better, and I didn't want anything else. I didn't want to get involved with anyone, fall in love again or have a family. And then I met you. And even though I knew I was getting in too deep, I couldn't stop myself. For the first time in fifteen years, I felt happy. I didn't want to let that feeling go, but when you proposed, I went into panic mode. How could we get married? You'd want to have kids, and there was no way in hell I could go through that again. I couldn't do it to myself, to you, or to a baby. I couldn't go through all that pain again to have the same thing happen. I couldn't go through having another stillbirth. It would kill me. That's why I said no. It was never because I didn't love you; it was because, deep down, I knew that being with you would cause more heartache in the long run. I know you want kids eventually, and I simply can't do that. I didn't want to inflict all this on you.'

Adam blinked and rubbed his face. She was looking back at him, and the room was silent after the almost constant barrage of confessions.

'I knew it was a risk to tell you,' she said, picking at a nail. 'But so much has happened that you had to know. And at least you know now why I can't go through with this pregnancy. I can't have it happen again. I've already lost one baby, Adam. And then when I went for the consultation, they told me that I'd been carrying twins, and one of them died. I can't do all that again.'

The hairs on the back of his neck stood on end, and every nerve in his body tingled as he tried to hold onto everything she'd told him. Blood pounded in his ears, and a vein pulsed with his heartbeat in his throat. His insides felt like they were shaking.

'I can't do this.' He shook his head, and before he could stop himself, he stood up, tightened the belt of his towelling robe and walked out of the room.

37.

Adam slammed the door to his hotel room behind him and made his way down the fire-escape stairs, two at a time. He'd dressed in record time, pulling on his damp suit, ignoring the way it clung to his skin. As he stepped outside the hotel, he took in a deep lungful of air. He'd felt suffocated in Sarah's room, but thanks to the thoughts careening through his head, he felt decidedly dizzy. He needed to walk, to try to clear his head.

He looked towards the shiny, regenerated part of the city centre and the twinkling lights illuminating the buildings ahead. It would be easy enough to find a pub where he could sit and sink into the bottom of a pint glass, surrounded by the buzz of conversation and the clunking of balls being knocked around a pool table. Instead, he turned right, down a street occupied by fried chicken shops and off-licences. Clearly the regeneration hadn't made it this far, and with the yellow street lights bouncing off the shuttered shopfronts, he could almost draw a line and pinpoint where the old city ended and the new one began. He dug his hands into his trouser pockets and kept his eyes on the road ahead. He had to stop himself from delving into the part of his mind where Sarah's confession had burrowed. He couldn't start thinking about what she'd told him yet.

As he walked up the road, he frowned, sniffing the air. It smelled like sweet onions, and he looked at the buildings around him, trying to work out where it was coming from. It reminded him of the pickled onions Sarah liked. He couldn't think of anything worse to eat, but she loved them.

He couldn't get out of his head the image of her face as she'd sat opposite him and told him about Jack. His stomach sank. So much for trying not to think about it. No way had he been expecting to hear that. Even when she'd told him she'd been pregnant before, he'd expected to hear that she'd given the baby up for adoption. It was as if she were talking about someone else entirely. A teenage delinquent who'd got pregnant at the age of fourteen and secretly given birth to and abandoned a stillborn baby. No wonder she was so secretive.

Adam clenched his jaw. The thought of what had happened to her was making his blood curdle. She really did do a mighty ostrich impression, like Claire had said. He shook his head. Why did she do all that – hide her pregnancy from everyone and go through it all alone – when she really didn't have to? Okay, she was scared of telling her mum; he could understand that, but to go to that extreme? He'd met her family, and they weren't the dragons she'd painted them to be. They almost certainly wouldn't have been happy about her being pregnant at such a young age, but whose parents would be?

It was blisteringly cold. The wind had dropped, but the bitter air around him nipped at his ears and stung his eyes, making them water. Everything around him looked so brown and soulless, and the road ahead stretched out for what seemed like forever. He'd only seen two cars drive past, and he hadn't seen anyone else since he'd left the hotel. His footsteps echoed around him, and the smell of onions still wafted in the air. Being alone suited him just fine. He didn't want to see anyone else or listen to the babble of conversation – not when he still had the one with Sarah replaying in his mind. The thought of her cradling the body of her newborn baby in her arms made him feel sick. No wonder she was so afraid about being pregnant again. Her reasons for wanting the abortion were clear to him now. If he'd known, he wouldn't have even raised the possibility of her keeping it as an option.

It? He shook his head. She'd said she had been pregnant with twins. She had really said that, hadn't she? She'd slipped it in, right at the end, and now he wasn't sure whether he'd heard correctly because his thoughts had been racing through his head with the revelations she'd told him. That would be three babies, and not one of them would have survived – through choice or fate. Something like that could mess with the strongest of minds.

He came to a bridge and stopped to look down at the brown water rushing against the mildew-ridden walls of its banks. He would never have imagined that he'd have a conversation like that three months ago. Hell, even a few hours ago. And what was worse, he didn't know how he was supposed to feel. He was sad for her – of course he was. Nobody should have to go through what she'd gone through, at any age – let alone as a teenager. The idea of Sarah and Claire doing what they did and hiding a secret of such magnitude for so many years was inconceivable to him. He didn't know what he was supposed to say to her, or what she expected to hear. Everything she'd said was on repeat in his head, and he kept running through the same thoughts like a paused video, stuttering and jumping, unable to move backwards or forwards.

It must have been the same for Sarah, stuck for the last fifteen years on the floor of a clapped-out cricket pavilion with her twin sister and a dead baby in her arms. It was a miracle she hadn't gone mad, keeping a secret like that to herself. It was a shocking thing for him to hear, but he was proud of her for telling him. Putting aside the impact it could have on their relationship, after years of shutting herself away, she'd faced up to her demons and laid them out for him to see. She thought she was weak, but all he could see was how amazingly strong she was.

Looking up, he saw the sign of their hotel in the distance. She'd probably be thinking all sorts of things, reading into the reasons why he'd walked out instead of staying, but he'd needed to take in what she'd told him in his own time, and he couldn't do that with her there. He rubbed his eyes before jamming his hands into his pockets and walking back to the hotel. He knew what he needed to do.

38.

10 November, 11.50 p.m.

Well, that's it. I've told him everything. I poured my heart out to him for what felt like hours and now there's nothing more to say. After keeping it locked inside for so long, I thought it would be the most painful thing in the world to admit to what happened. To finally tell the truth about Jack and come—

❧

Sarah stopped writing and looked up at the door. Someone was there – she was sure of it. She gripped the pen in her hand. What if it was the police? What if that was the reason Adam had walked out? The look on his face when she'd told him everything made no secret about what he thought. It was a look of pure horror and disgust, and he'd probably gone straight to the nearest police station.

A knock at the door confirmed her thoughts, and a pulse of fear ran down her back. She'd known when she'd made the decision to tell Adam everything that this might happen. She hadn't expected to confess to something like that without consequences, and him walking out was just one of them.

'Sarah?'

He knocked again and her breath quickened. Why had he come back?

'You know, I would have understood if you'd told me all this before,' Adam said. 'I wouldn't have thought any differently about you. You know that, don't you?'

Sarah frowned. Of course he would have. How could he not? The words he was saying didn't match up with what his face had told her before he'd walked out.

'What happened wasn't your fault.' He looked up, straight into the spyhole. There was no way he could have seen her or even known she was there, but it was as if he were looking right at her. 'You didn't know you were pregnant – you can't blame yourself for what happened. And even if you did know, it might have ended the same way. There might not have been anything you could've done.'

Tears pricked at her eyes, and she stepped away from the door. If it wasn't her fault, then whose was it? Miscarriages and stillbirths happened all the time; she knew that. She'd spent years repeatedly going back to support websites and reading reports published in medical journals. She knew that sometimes there *was* no explanation. But it didn't make it any easier. If she had nobody to blame, then she'd have to live with the knowledge that, for some reason, it was just never meant to be.

'Look, Sarah. I know you're there. I know you're listening.'

Her heart thudded so loudly, she was sure he'd be able to hear it on the other side of the door. She looked at the spyhole and pictured Adam on the other side.

'I still want you. I still want *us*. I want us to be a family, and I think you do too.'

The tears rolled from her eyes and down her cheeks. Even now that he knew everything there was to know, he was still there, wanting her. She peered through the spyhole again, looking at him.

'If you want to make this work, then we'll do it,' Adam said. 'No more secrets, no more lies. I know you're scared, but things will be different this time around.'

Her stomach turned with the weight of his words. What he was asking her to do was impossible. They'd have to start all over again, trying to piece back together what they'd had, and they'd have to do it with a baby.

'And, if you don't . . .' He put his forehead against the door and sighed. 'If you don't, then I'll drop it.'

What if it didn't work out?

'All you have to do is open the door and tell me what you want. What do you want, Sarah?'

EPILOGUE

Adam kicked the door shut behind him after taking the brown paper bags from the delivery man, and headed into the kitchen. Thank God for Fridays. He was looking forward to tucking into his lamb bhuna and chilling in front of the TV. It was hardly rock and roll, but after the last few months of complications and drama, it was exactly what he needed. His stomach growled as he took a beer from the fridge. He looked up at the clock, shrugged and peeled the lid off his lamb. One spoonful wouldn't hurt.

With the kick of the chilli tingling his lips, Adam took a swig of his beer. No doubt Matt and Jenny would be sitting around Carl's huge dining table in the middle of a poker game. It still felt odd not to be there. After years of maintaining that it was an absolute staple of his life, he hadn't been for weeks, but now his world had changed, and his rule that 'Girls can come and go, but poker night remains' had gone straight out of the window.

'Finally,' Adam said as he heard the front door open.

'Bloody hell, it's pissing it down out there,' Sarah shouted from the hallway. 'Is the food here? I'm starving.'

'Sit down and chill. I'll be two secs.'

He gathered up two trays, plates and cutlery, all the while listening to the noises of Sarah moving around the flat – something that always made him smile. He tore off some sheets from the roll of kitchen paper and turned off the light before remembering the can of ginger beer in the fridge that he'd picked up for her on the way home.

He held out the tray in front of him. 'Here you go.'

She'd already selected a film from the on-demand service. Which soppy chick flick was it going to be this time? *Amelie?* It was her favourite film, and he knew for a fact that she'd seen it at least a dozen times. He had to admit he liked it too, even if it was all in subtitles. He sat down next to her on the sofa and looked at her, balancing her tray on her knees. He smiled to himself. Who needed poker nights anyway?

⁓

'Ow.'

'Is everything okay?' Adam asked, his eyebrows rising with alarm.

'Yeah, she's just moving around a bit.'

He breathed a sigh of relief and looked down at Sarah's swollen belly. It wasn't time for him to start panicking about overnight hospital bags and the possibility of a backseat delivery just yet.

He still found it hard to believe there was a baby growing inside her. Their baby. Adam smiled – a smile he'd been unable to wipe off his face since Sheffield. He was going to be a dad. For real. Another person was going to be reliant on him for her welfare. He was excited – ecstatic, even. And terrified. He'd wake up sometimes in the middle of the night, wondering how the hell they were going to cope with the demands of a baby.

'Do you want to feel?' Sarah asked. 'She's kicking up a storm.'

Adam hesitated. So far, whenever he'd put his hand to Sarah's belly, he'd never felt anything. It was almost like his daughter was playing games with him, already showing her stubborn side. Clearly, she took after her mum.

'She'll probably stop if I do.'

'Don't be so ridiculous,' she replied, flicking her eyes to the ceiling, and grabbed his hand.

The hardness of her belly still astounded him, and every so often, he'd see it move. It creeped him out the first time. He'd expected it to be a slight ripple, but instead, he'd actually seen a lump form as the baby moved under Sarah's skin.

Adam shrugged. 'I can't feel anything.'

'Here,' Sarah replied, lifting her top and pressing his palm against her warm, bare skin. 'Just wait a few seconds.'

He sighed, shaking his head. It was useless. He was never going to feel her kick. He was about to move his hand, when a sharp, sudden and firm kick nudged against his skin.

His stomach somersaulted and his eyebrows shot up. 'Was that it?'

'Yep,' Sarah nodded. 'Pretty amazing, huh?'

He nodded back and kept his hand where it was. Amazing was one word to describe it, that was for sure. He'd been to the second ultrasound scan and seen their baby on the screen. He'd heard its heartbeat, and when Sarah had looked at him with the sonar-like pulse of the heartbeat echoing around the room, he knew that she was thinking about the baby they'd lost, just as he was. The happiness of hearing their baby's heartbeat was tinged with sadness for the one that hadn't survived, and they'd gone home to read up about vanishing twin syndrome. They were still mourning their loss, and he guessed they always would, but at the same time, they'd moved on to a point where the overwhelming emotion they seemed to share was happiness.

'She's actually real.'

Sarah laughed. 'Of course she is. Do you think I've been walking around with a pillow stuffed under my top all this time?'

Adam shook his head and took his hand from her bump to rub his mouth. Now that he'd felt it move, his daughter had gone from being a conceptual being to an actual one. 'No, it's just . . . Well, it's a big deal.'

Sarah looked at him and smiled. 'Yeah, it is.'

'Will she move again?' he asked, flicking his gaze from Sarah's belly to her eyes. The movement had been so quick and sudden that he hadn't felt prepared for it. He wanted to feel it again.

'Probably,' she replied and took his hand again. 'She seems to love jalfrezi as much as I do.'

'We'll have to get some more curry in next weekend then. Your mum will want to feel that for sure.'

Sarah smiled. Having Caroline and Peter come to stay for the weekend was her idea, to try to start rebuilding the relationship with her family. Ever since she'd told them she was pregnant, she seemed to be on the phone to her mum on a daily basis.

Adam took her hand and looked at her. 'What about Amy?'

Sarah scrunched up her nose. 'I'm not keen. I like Jessica. Or Emily.'

'I don't like either of those.' Adam frowned. 'Not having much luck so far, are we?'

Sarah shrugged and grinned. 'We've got plenty of time.'

She was right. They had a whole future mapping itself out ahead of them. The two of them, with a daughter. A girl who would throw tantrums, play with dolls, wear makeup and eventually bring all manner of worries to Adam's head with dodgy boyfriends. He couldn't wait.

Sarah put her hand over his, and they both waited for the second kick. Whatever challenges their daughter would throw their way, he knew they would face them together. After everything they'd been through, they were even stronger than before. They were back together, and in a couple of weeks, they would be a family.

'I've been thinking,' Adam said, gently stroking his thumb against Sarah's soft skin.

'Hurt, did it?'

'Funny.' He rolled his eyes at Sarah's cheeky grin. 'So, on the subject of names, maybe it's better to wait until she's born. You know, to see what she looks like.'

Sarah nodded. 'Okay. That works for me. As long as you don't try and take advantage of my post-natal haze and get me to agree to calling her Arsenal or something.'

'Scout's honour.' Adam laughed.

'On the topic of names, we're agreed her surname will be Thompson, right?'

Adam nodded. 'Right.'

'Well, I was thinking that it would be really nice if we *all* shared it.'

Shared his surname? A puzzled frown settled on Adam's face. Things were going well between them – fantastic, actually – but even still. He'd learned not to assume anything over the past few months.

'What are you saying?'

'Marry me, Adam.'

ACKNOWLEDGEMENTS

Writing *Together Apart* has been a huge journey, and I owe a big thanks to Caroline Batten for reading, rereading, encouragement and much-needed reality checks; and to Janny Peacock, Jo Gardner and Gemma Harris for all the lengthy chats that kept me sane. Thanks also to Sam Curniffe and Thandi Davis, my very own PR machines. A huge thanks to everyone in the Authonomy community who commented on and voted for the early versions of *Together Apart*, and enormous thanks to my Wattpad followers – you guys rock!

Thank you also to the great team of editors at Amazon, particularly Emilie for seeing the potential of *Together Apart*, and Sophie for pushing the edits to make it even better than it was.

Finally, thanks to you, the readers, without whom *Together Apart* would be pointless. I hope you fell in love with Adam and Sarah as much as I did.

ABOUT THE AUTHOR

Photo © 2014 Natalie K Martin

Natalie K Martin is a lover of books, music and chocolate peanuts. Originally from Sheffield, Natalie is based in London and loves all things French. In January 2014, she decided to leave her job and travel to India where she published her debut novel, *Together Apart*. Since her return to the UK, her feet have been itching to go somewhere else.

Join Natalie's mailing list for details about upcoming releases and – if you fancy getting signed copies of her books, exclusive content and swag – join her street team, The Circle, on www.nataliekmartin.com.

For more info, you can contact Natalie via her website and blog, www.nataliekmartin.com; on Twitter, @natkmartin; and on Facebook, www.facebook.com/nataliemartinauthor.